The Byworlder

The Worlds of Poul Anderson

The Night Face and Other Stories
The Byworlder
The Horn of Time
The Long Way Home
Orbit Unlimited
The Queen of Air and Darkness
Two Worlds

The Byworlder

By POUL ANDERSON

With a New Introduction by the Author

BOSTON

GREGG PRESS

1978

Library of Congress Cataloging in Publication Data

Anderson, Poul, 1926-
The byworlder.

(The worlds of Poul Anderson)
Reprint of the ed. published by New American
Library, New York, in series: A Signet book.
I. Title. II. Series: Anderson, Poul, 1926-
The worlds of Poul Anderson.
PZ4.A549By   1978   [PS3551.N378]   813'.5'4
ISBN 0-8398-2432-7

Introduction

M Y BELIEF is that a book should speak for itself. If it needs any comment by the author, than he or she has failed. A partial exception may occur when *additional* material, not integral to the story, is of interest. For example, a historical novelist may discuss his sources, a science fiction writer may go into greater detail about his imagined setting than the narrative allows, or anybody may wax philosophical or anecdotal. In a small way, the last of these is all that I can do for *The Byworlder*.

Futuristic tales reflect the times in which they were written as much as do any other kinds of fiction. Consider such of the works of H. G. Wells as fall into that category. (Wells' works are always worth considering, anyway. Except for Rudyard Kipling, whose ventures into science fiction were few and short, the field has yet to see a better writer within the English language.) The world which the narrator of *The Time Machine* visits, thousands of years hence, is a projection of the late Victorian stage of industrialism, with emphasis on the often cruel class distinctions of contemporary England. The world of *Men Like Gods*—technically in a parallel universe, but actually a utopia which Wells claimed we could attain ourselves—has sources as seemingly diverse, yet really convergent, as William Morris and Algernon Charles Swinburne; Isadora Duncan stood, and danced, for the same basic ideal. Wells' "A Dream of Armageddon," one of the most chilling short stories ever written, describes a collapse of civilization through war and revolution that would, in fact, soon occur in several parts of the world, and was already being foreseen by a few thinkers. I could go on, but this seems enough to make the point.

Of course, science fiction often draws on past history, however the author transmutes this. Nevertheless, the author is still looking through his own time-bound eyes. The future barbarisms in Jack London's *The Scarlet Plague* and George Stewart's *Earth Abides*, to

1

name two outstanding cases, are explicitly shown as having roots in the present. Even when the present has been essentially forgotten, as in Stephen Vincent Benét's "By the Waters of Babylon," the discoveries the hero makes, the experiences he has, the very thoughts he thinks, are those that will most appeal to a 20th-century reader. A classical Greek or Chinese, imagining such a situation, would have told quite a different story. Likewise, though some science fiction draws close parallels to past events—Isaac Asimov's *Foundation* series being doubtless the most famous case—we don't really get the Roman Empire, or Byzantium, or the Hanseatic League, or whatever, in thin disguise. It isn't possible. For that matter, I wonder how faithful to its setting the most carefully researched and deeply empathetic historical novel, such as Sigrid Undset's *Kristin Lavransdatter*, can really be.

The Byworlder, a fairly straightforward extrapolation into the near future, offers a case in point of all the foregoing. Time has not yet caught up with it, as time did long ago with books like G. K. Chesterton's *The Flying Inn* (which remains eminently worth reading just the same). Already, though, the years give sufficient perspective on it so that, even without a copyright notice to go on, a perceptive reader could still estimate pretty closely when it was written. According to my records, it was shipped off to my agent on 16 April 1970, seeing print about a year later. This means it was in the typewriter for some months preceding, and I'd been thinking seriously about it for a while before that—which gets us back to 1969.

Add to this the fact that I live in a suburb of the Berkeley, California area, have many friends in that city, and frequently have other occasions to visit it, especially the University and environs. Thus, while no partaker myself, I was a close witness of what happened there, as the old Berkeley Bohemians gave way in succession to the beatniks, the hippies, the activists, the revolutionaries, and at last, for the time being, a sort of quietism which is in no way identical with any earlier state of affairs.

Not to preach a sermon but merely to identify a viewpoint, let me remark that my ideas have evolved, or at least changed, in various respects over the decades, but they have always involved commitment to individual liberty. It and the scientific method are the two great contributions to humanity of post-medieval Western civilization. Most societies have no interest in either liberty or scientific method. This is not necessarily bad; cultural diversity is a major source of progress, besides adding to life's fascination. His own ideal forbids the libertarian to call a crusade against anybody else. However, his ideal does not forbid him to defend it; and today more than one powerful government is implacably hostile to liberty and intends to expunge it from Earth as fast and thoroughly as possible.

Since the United States of America is the last serious defender the West, and liberty, have left, and since the American bourgeoisie, who include most blue collar workers, are the last backbone the United States has left, it follows that these are the prime targets of hatred, vilification, and violence on the part of those who desire a collectivist order of things. Anarchists, too, are mostly adverse, though not always nor often as extremely. (By and large, their hearts are in the right place, and they simply haven't thought the matter through.) Thus I found myself, privately and sometimes publicly, ranged against the whole hodgepodge of radical movements, and got the reputation of being quite a Tory.

In a way, *The Byworlder* was written as a denial of that. Not that it was intended to clear my name—Toryism is perfectly respectworthy in both moral and intellectual terms—nor to convert anybody to my opinions or any such dismal objective. It's merely that reflection upon what was going on around me became a wellspring of the story.

After all, I'd been concerned about what we're doing to nature long before this was fashionable. As far back as 1950, I'd published a novelette, "The Helping Hand," which was an out-and-out parable about the dangers in trying to Americanize all mankind. I'd tried various ways of living and meant to continue doing so. I had close friends whose philosophies and private arrangements were utterly different from mine but who, in an atmosphere of mutual courtesy, had much to teach me. I was aware of the problem of anomie and, indeed, considered it a deep root of alienation and hence of revolutionism; Eric Hoffer had analyzed that brilliantly. The overgrowth of domestic government was stifling me too. And so on.

At the same time, there were elements of hopefulness. By sheer productivity, modern industrial civilization can support such a tremendous diversity of enterprises that, given official tolerance and a willingness to forego a certain amount of material wealth, any reasonably intelligent and energetic person can already pretty well shape his or her own life. That opportunity did not exist in the farming community where I spent my youth; it would have been contrasurvival, just as genuine equality of the sexes would have been. Today, on the contrary, the specialization and mechanization of the truly essential jobs are *forcing* more and more people to strike out on their own. Occasionally they do this in cooperative style, even in communes, and what's wrong with that if all the members are there voluntarily? Utopian experiments are a part of the American tradition.

Maybe these trends would continue, while more ominous trends declined, until at last, within the seemingly rigid framework of managerial society, we had a huge population of . . . byworlders. That would by no means create a paradise, but in several respects it might make for more freedom and happiness than we enjoy today.

Of course, I wasn't predicting this. It merely struck me as a possibility worth exploring. One unspoken postulate was the availability of cheap, abundant energy. Now we are hearing about an "energy crisis," the necessity of "lowered expectations," and all the rest. It could well prove to be a self-fulfilling prophecy, but in fact it's only the latest rhetoric of the collectivists and neo-Puritans. No doubt many problems and some hardships lie ahead at best. Yet if we hang onto common sense we can get through, and end up materially better off than ever. Nuclear fusion, orbiting solar collectors, oceanic temperature differentials, conversion of plants (specially developed for the purpose) to alcohol fuel, are four ways off a long list. As for mineral resources and sites for industry where it won't harm Earth, why, we have the whole of space.

Still, if I were writing this book today, I'd spell that out more clearly. I might also pay more attention to the problems of women; as is, a remark by a male character, not by me, with no malice on his part or mine, seems to have outraged a few ultra-feminists. Well, though a science fiction writer may luck out once in a while and "forecast" a little of the technology and even a little of the social structure of tomorrow's world, there is no way he can guess its preoccupations.

I haven't much else to say. The visitor from Outside is present partly to be the nucleus of the plot, partly because I wanted to try my hand at creating a nonhuman who really was nonhuman, through and through. My success or failure in that is for you, the reader, to judge. So is the success or failure of the book as a whole. I hope it will at least entertain you.

POUL ANDERSON

I

———◆———

The ship from Sigma in the Dragon had changed orbit, inexplicably as always. Now it circled close, barely above atmosphere, a star which newscasts around the world said would rise before dawn. Many folk must have wondered, must have been a little hopeful or a little afraid; but probably few got up to witness the sight. Three blank years had somewhat blunted awe.

That did not seem to be the case in We. The coming of the ship had been more for the Theontologists than a spiritual event. Everything was supposed to be that. It had brought on a kind of spiritual crisis. Finally they integrated the ship's existence with the formal part of their religion, and the sole telescreen in We was monitored largely for whatever word might come in about it.

One among those who had spent the night in vigil blew on a conch to awaken the rest. The lowing roused Skip, too, where he slept on a pallet in the room of Urania's two small boys. He yawned, muttered a drowsy "Damn," and climbed from under his blankets. Adobe makes good insulation, but the nights get cold in northwest New Mexico and the window stood open. He shivered. The air was dry in his nostrils, faintly sweetened by sagebrush smoke. He turned on the fluoros, glad he didn't have to fumble around with candles. This community might believe in the simple life, but it had the common sense to realize how simplicity depended on a selective use of technics. "Tom Swift and his electric Tibet," he had said to himself on first arriving here.

The room leaped forth in the light—handmade furniture, an outsize God's Eye hung on a whitewashed wall. Urania belonged to the Spirits cult. But she or somebody had also made humanly foolish toys for the children, and half-finished on another wall was the mural of fairytale characters that Skip was painting. This colony didn't seem

5

to hold more than the usual proportion of stuffed shirts. Maybe less, in fact. He had been received with cheer as well as warmth.

His packsack held one good suit, dark-blue tunic and pants in the Timeless style. He didn't carry curly-toed buskins around, though, just a change of walking shoes. Passing into the main room, he found Sandalphon and Urania. The man, who was tall and richly bearded, belonged to the Jesus cult and had thus donned a black ceremonial robe, setting off a pectoral cross of turquoise-studded silver. The woman's slight form was almost lost in an Indian blanket; Skip glimpsed an ankle-length beaded gown beneath.

"Blessings," Sandalphon greeted. "I'm sorry the call interrupted your sleep."

Is that a hint? "Uh, I figured I'd tail along," Skip answered. "But of course, if you'd rather not have outsiders—or if you want a babysitter—"

"Nonsense!" Urania squeezed his hand. "Nothing to fear. The boys will still be tucked in when we come back. And as for the ceremonies, this is a general observance—no in-cult secrets—and you are welcome." Her pert features kindled with a smile. "Why, we might convert you."

Likelihood not bloody, Skip thought. He ducked into the bathroom. Combing his hair took little time. He wore it short, bobbed directly under the ears, to save trouble. Or at least he minimized trouble; the brown locks always seemed to go their own ways after about five minutes. He was likewise an individualist in being clean-shaven, though that was because, at age twenty-two, he couldn't yet raise a crop of whiskers which wouldn't look as if locusts had been in it. (*Hey, a cartoon idea there.*) Otherwise he was in appearance ordinary: medium height; rather stocky; however, more agile than most; freckled face, snub nose, large green eyes.

Returning, he found Sandalphon and Urania benched at the rough plank table in the kitchen. An incense stick smoked near a teapot and three cups. Outside, the conch had been joined by a gong. Skip wondered how the kids could sleep, then decided they must be used to chanting and such at odd hours. Urania laid finger on lips and motioned him to sit. Sandalphon traced a cross in the air; she kept her gaze downward into her cup. The tea was drunk with slow ceremoniousness. It was hot, pungent, a trifle dizzying. *Probably some pot in the pot*, Skip thought.

When they were finished, Urania stopped on the way

out and draped a necklace of miscellaneous shells over her guest's shoulders. No doubt each had a meaning. He'd been surprised at first by the elaborateness of ritual and symbolism in We. The village was only about ten years old. For that matter, the original preachings of what was to become Theontology had been less than three decades ago. Soon he realized that most was adapted from ancient traditions. "Our apprehension of reality is largely the construct of our own minds," Joswick wrote. "Thus anything ever imagined has truth in it, partial and distorted; it is a sign among many pointing toward that cosmic oneness we call God. Through meditation upon all these aspects, conventional and unconventional religion, myth, science, philosophy, art, all we can experience, we open our beings and may in the end hope for direct apprehension of the divine."

With frugality, hard work, and endless devotional exercises, We therefore combined ecstatic states and occasionally orgiastic rites. Withdrawn from the modern world, it nonetheless practiced up-to-date dry farming with the latest gene-tailored plants; it turned out handicrafts shrewdly designed to sell at good prices in big-city stores; and few of its dwellers seemed intolerant of anything that outsiders might choose to do.

A nice bunch, Skip thought. *Rather too george for me. I won't be staying long, especially if none of the alices will give me a gallop. But I'm glad I came.*

Urania took him by the hand. His pulses leaped. He was a bit in love with her. Of course, he was nearly always a bit in love with somebody.

They emerged in the single unpaved street. The adobes shouldered black against a sky still dark, still wild with crystalline stars and Milky Way. At the far end of the street, leaders were assembling their groups by a bonfire. Lanterns swayed and glowed, picking out banners, rosaries, costumes, rapt countenances, the thousand-odd adults and older children. Their feet shuffled loud in the murk, their breath smoked white in the crackling cold.

Sandalphon left to join those whose cult-lodge-token was of Jesus. Urania led Skip toward three masked, feathered dancers at the head of the Spirits' people. Their tom-toms had begun to mutter. On the way, he saw the variously clad ones who chose to seek God in Brahma, Amida Butsu, Snake, Oracle. Flute, lyre, and Gregorian chant came into the music, which somehow remained a harmonious whole. The lanterns were extinguished. In seven columns, the last for postulants, the villagers passed slowly onto the Nason's Peak trail.

The moon was down, but starlight touched gray-white vistas of cultivated fields slanting toward a stream where cottonwoods grew, of sagebrush elsewhere, boulders, a scuttering jackrabbit, a ghosting owl, majestic mountains. Skip felt his irreverent heart uplifted. The night was so huge and holy.

A half hour's climb gained the top. Here stood that altar block inscribed "To the Unknown God." The people of We placed themselves behind it, faced west, and were silent.

The spacecraft rose, and a long soft "O-o-o-oh!" broke forth.

Skip had seen the sight before, when the ship happened to be similarly near Earth. It was an endless marvel and joy to him—that beings beyond the sky had made the abyss come alive by sending an emissary in *his* lifetime. That the envoy should be so strange that three years of struggle to reach understanding only deepened bewilderment in the best minds mankind had to offer, was to him exciting, a challenge, maybe even someday a chance for him.

This hour before dawn he stood among a thousand who had come to believe that the traveler from Sigma Draconis must be a direct manifestation of God; and the coldness of the mountain night ran along his spine.

The twinkling light-point swung rapidly higher among the constellations. Skip wasn't sure whether or not he could make out the accompanying module. A few binocular lenses shimmered wan in his sight. He didn't quite dare ask to borrow. Those folk were looking on a persona of their ultimate.

"*Hail . . . Ave . . . Om mani padme hum . . .*" The chants, the dances, the kneelings and prostrations commenced. They went on after the ship had vanished in the paling eastern heaven. Skip stood aside.

Worship ended, cult by cult. In simple unorganized fashion, the community straggled back to breakfast. Some chatted, some walked silent. The east whitened, the land came awake with light.

Skip found himself again accompanying Urania. "Where's Sandalphon?" he asked.

She blinked long-lashed eyes at him. A breeze stirred the hairs which had strayed from her ruddy braids. "Didn't you know? I'm sorry. He and I must each have assumed the other told you. He's been arranging to go on a month's retreat, and decided to make this the occasion of starting."

So lost in the landscape lay We that Skip must laugh. "A hermitage from that?"

She smiled in turn. Outside her orisons, and to a large extent inside them, she was a relaxed and unaffected young woman. No name change upon being received into the kiva of the Spirits could wipe out little Mary Peterson, who had once felt hollow and unhappy in Chicago. "Takes all kinds, hm? Like you. I'm curious about you, more maybe than you are about me."

He shrugged. "You've heard the official facts. Not much to them."

In the first stage of acquaintance, when she asked about him, he had said: "Thomas John Wayburn, always called Skip, I don't know why. Born and raised in Berkeley, California, comfortable middle class, father an electronics engineer, mother a computer programmer. Brother and sister stayed george. None of them are overjoyed at having a sigaroon in the family, but we aren't estranged either. I see them now and then."

"A . . . what?"

"George. Staid taxpayer type. . . . Oh. You mean sigaroon? I suppose it is a newish bit of argot at that. A drifter." In haste: "Not a grifter. We have our standards— well, nothing like a fraternity exists, we only kind of think alike, live alike, junction up together when we meet—we don't beg, bully, or steal. Whoever does soon finds the rest won't have any further to do with him, if only to protect their own good name. You see, we're migratory workers, dependent on being trusted."

"I've heard about those, naturally. But you talk as if a lot more have taken up that life since I came here. Can they really find work?"

"You'd be surprised. Sure, machines are doing most of the harvesting as well as manufacturing these days. But you'd be surprised what a demand there is for odd jobs done, personal services, entertainment that doesn't come out of a tube. And, uh, we're not clinkerbrains. Some of us have college educations. I was offered a scholarship. But I didn't want to be tied down, anyway not before I'd tasted a lot of the world, so I went on the wing. If you didn't want me to decorate that room we've been talking about, well, I'm a pretty fair carpenter, mechanic, repairman, gardener, et cetera, and I have songs to sing and stories to tell."

She had nodded thoughtfully, her gaze gone far away, as she remembered what she had left. "I see," she murmured. "Modern material productivity can support almost any class of persons, any style of existence."

"Plenty of money floating around, for sure. I haven't yet had to exercise my right to a public works billet. That's a common stunt, though—do cleanup or whatever for just half a year. You can then get by at liberty for the next six months, if your wants are few."

"Right. Please understand that this community doesn't disdain cybernation and machines. Without them—without income guarantee, the low price of most necessities, cheap and versatile power tools, everything technology makes possible—I doubt we could have made a go of this." She had gestured at We around her.

Now she asked: "Did you really come here for no other purpose than to see what it's like?"

"I told you that when I arrived, Urania," he answered. "I'm a subculture hopper. The subcultures are springing up like mushrooms." He frowned. "Poison toadstools among them. But plenty of good clean mushrooms, like here."

She giggled. "What a compliment! Calling me a mushroom."

"Why, uh—" Confused, he blushed.

She took his arm, pressing it against her side. "Don't be so teasable. I want to know you better. A lot better. That's why Sandalphon decided to leave this soon."

He stopped. His heart sprang. "You . . . you mean—?"

"Yes, I do mean," she said frankly. "We don't observe formal marriage. Too much chance of complications, jealousy, a dozen kinds of distraction from the spirit. But celibacy is worse yet, isn't it?"

They kissed. The sun rose blindingly over a tall peak. A lark whistled. A few persons in sight voiced friendly cheers.

After a while Urania stepped back, flushed and breathing hard. "That's another thing you're good at, boy," she said.

"And you." Actually, she seemed naive compared to some—how many altogether, since he was fourteen?—but maybe she was shy in public, and anyhow it didn't matter, he was in love again for a time and he had a job he enjoyed and though shadows were long and blue the air had already warmed enough to bring him a sweetness of sage.

They continued downhill, hand in hand but faster than before, dancing and laughing. When they reached Urania's house, she must first ready her youngsters for school. We avoided trouble with state education authorities by keeping its own certified teachers of required subjects. Ample hours remained for Theontology.

Urania whispered she'd arranged yesterday to have today off from her share of communal labor. He needn't faunch. Besides, breakfast would be mighty welcome!

"I wanted to see the spaceship," Micah said.

His mother rumpled his hair. "Too early for you, dear. It looks like any artificial satellite."

He clouded for a storm. "I *want* to!"

"That's a wrong attitude. You're turning inward from God."

"Aw, he's only six," Skip said. "Mike, I mean, not God. I think you can see it Saturday, fella, if it's hung around. Right? Now c'mon, you bucks, get washed and dressed and I'll tell you a story while the pancakes are making."

"A Maroon Balloon story," Joel demanded at once, for Skip always made him the hero of those.

"A story 'bout the planet Willoughby," Micah said for similar reasons.

"No time for both," Skip pointed out. "I'll tell you about a, uh, a dragon."

While they splashed and shouted and became more or less presentable, he sat at the kitchen table, his attention half on a Urania moving about more sensuously than hitherto, half on the sketch pad he used to illustrate while he related. *A dragon . . . what about a dragon?* He drew it potbellied and smug-looking, so much that he put a halo above. *A most pious dragon.* Bible clutched under the right forepaw. *In fact, a saint dragon. No. Better not. Might spoil her mood.* He changed the Bible to a piece of sheet music, wrote *"O sole mio"* in what had been the halo, and the story became that of Philibert Phiredrake, who wanted to sing on the concert stage but kept setting it aflame until two clever boys named Joel and Micah thought to install a hood, whose pipe led to a Dutch oven where the dragon's dinner could be cooked. Telling it gave him small opportunity to eat before the half-brothers had scampered out.

He reached for Urania, who dodged. "Don't paw my

clean floor," she said merrily. "I want a proper meal in you. We've the entire day and night, you know." She had told the kids to stay elsewhere till next morning. Such favors were casually exchanged. Doing away with the nuclear family had its advantages, Skip reflected, though he knew that presently he would find the togetherness of We stifling.

She started to cook for him. He sipped his coffee. Sunlight poured through the open window, soaked into mellow earth walls, glowed on a kachina pattern. Fragrance welled from the stove. She was right, he confessed; his belly was growling. Otherwise the walk had invigorated him. He felt gigantic with happiness.

"That was quite a yarn," Urania said. "I don't see how you can do it on the spur of the moment. They'll miss you when you go."

"Oh, it's nothing special," he said, touched by quick unease.

She sobered, didn't look his way, busied her hands. "I'll miss you too," she said low. "You wouldn't consider staying?"

"I wouldn't fit in. Not the religious type."

"Everybody is, at heart. That's why society is breaking in pieces. . . . Yes, it is. The Ortho grows more and more frantic, hunting for pleasure, novelty, thrills, anything to numb the pain of being empty. I belonged to the Ortho myself, remember; I know. And what makes the rest break away altogether, turn their backs on the whole thing, try completely new ways to live or try to revive old ones from a past that never was? What except a search, a need, for meanings? Your sigaroons included, darling. You yourself."

"N-n-no, hardly me. I'm just an artist. I hope someday to be a good artist. That's the end of my ambitions." Skip rubbed his chin. He was not introspective by nature. "I think in the long run it'll turn out that going on the wing was right for me. Staying in a studio, reading books and gawping at TV, what does that give a buck to paint *about?*"

She did regard him. "I can't believe you weren't near God this dawn," she said.

Briefly a ghost of that eeriness returned. "Well . . . maybe. . . . Kind of like times I've camped out, lain in my sleeping bag and looked straight up at the stars. I'd feel what a whirling tiny ball the planet is, and us nothing more than specks and flickers on it. The feeling was scary and glorious." He retreated toward the everyday. "But shucks, lady, I can't stay solemn for more'n thirty seconds in a row."

She pursued. "The mystery, Skip. That being isn't merely a foreigner in costume. It's a creature, a ... an existence we can't comprehend. Don't you see, it shows us that science will never give more than a broken piece of understanding, even of what we can see and touch?"

The cakes were ready. She shoveled them onto his plate and sat down opposite him. He poured on molassess. *If I don't steer her off this missionary runway, it could be hours before she'll gallop. Maybe never, if she gets angry at me.* "M-m-m, what lovely proviant!" he said around a mouthful.

She sighed and reached across to stroke his hand. "I want you to win enlightenment. You deserve it."

"Not really. Look, robin, let me be honest. I respect your beliefs but they aren't mine. To me, the Sigman's behavior is, well, interesting. A problem they'll solve sooner or later. It obviously doesn't think like us, but would you expect a nonhuman to? Eventually some bright boy will find a key, and once we're through the door, I bet communication'll get established astonishingly fast."

"Unless it leaves first. Forever."

Skip nodded, his pleasure dimmed. That fear was voiced quite often as the months of bafflement mounted into years. Didn't the ship take frequent tours elsewhere, immense curves to sister planets, at speeds unmatchable by the puny craft of man's first half-century in space—yes, sometimes orbiting the sun itself, close enough for radiation to kill a human vessel—the human crew would long have been dead—wouldn't such a path at last reach, not back to Earth in weeks, but to Ginnungagap?

That technological miracles would go with it, out of man's grasp, was the smallest dread. The possibility of star travel had now been proven. But *this* generation would be denied it. Maybe the denial would outlive humankind. Skip, who always carried several paperback books and found odd moments for reading them, had seen more than one competent scientist's doubts whether machine civilization, confined to a single livable planet, would survive many centuries.

"I'm afraid that could be," he said. "How long can we expect the chap, alone the way he, she, or it is, getting nowhere at arranging a language with us, how long a heel-cooling can we reasonably expect?"

"The trouble is," Urania said, caught up by earnestness, "they're taking too limited an approach. Sending scientists mostly, a few officers and bureaucrats and journalists. Nobody else gets invited. Hasn't it occurred to anyone that perhaps what the Sigman wants isn't to communicate but commune?"

"Can you do the second without the first?" Skip resigned himself to a conversation which, if not in the main line of his immediate interest, need not be dull either. "What's occurred to me is, the Sigman may not really be interested in us. Polite, I suppose we must admit. But maybe having no motives, emotions, purposes in common with us. Though damn it, you'd think their being a species who build starships, like we hope to, you'd think that shows the reason for making the trip is one we could see. If—"

And his mouth fell open, his fork clattered to the table, he let out a yell which brought Urania scrambling frightened to her feet.

II

———◆———

After a week, the vessel returned to its usual Earth orbit. The manned satellites reported it was englobed for an hour in a rainbow ripple of luminance. That meant the Sigman would receive visitors: almost the sole signal which men believed they had unambiguously decoded. Because those welcomes never lasted more than a few days, spacecraft and personnel were kept on standby, according to schemes which had formerly been the subject of fierce scholarly and political wrangling. Nowadays assignments were made on a somewhat more rational basis.

Not that that said anything very noble about *Homo sapiens*, Yvonne Canter reflected. (Meanwhile she scrambled into a coverall, grabbed the bag she always kept packed, closed her apartment, took the elevator fifty floors down to the conurb's garage, set the pilot of her car for Armstrong Base, lit a cigarette, and tried to relax. She did not succeed.) Three years of frustration had drained most of the prestige, professional or international, out of being personally on the scene. Besides, everything that happened was fully recorded in every feasible way and put on the open data lines. You could mull it over in the comfort and privacy of your office and have as good a chance of getting a publishable paper as did the poor devils who'd sweated to gather such a maddeningly tiny and vague increment of information.

That's what they think, Yvonne told herself. *Doubtless they've been right hitherto. But this time, oh, this time, maybe—* The blood beat high within her.

The Denver streets were only thinly in use at five a.m. Traffic Control's computers steered the car out of town in short order. When their electronic writ no longer ran, the pilot opened fuel cells to maximum, till the electrics whined aloud, and made the 300-odd-kilometer run inside of ninety minutes. Yvonne hardly noticed the

15

flat agricultural landscape reel by, nor the sprawling complex through which she finally rolled.

The observation did cross a mind otherwise churning with plans: Not alone Armstrong, the working spaceport, had lost glamour. The same had happened to Kennedy's R & D—to all of man's astronautical facilities. With a starship overhead, you continued ferrying supplies to the Lunar and Martian stations, you continued organizing a Jupiter expedition, you spoke of sending men to Saturn; but your heart wasn't in it.

She came back to alertness when she sat before Colonel Almeida's desk for briefing. Liftoff was set at 9:45; she'd arrive first by two hours— "I forget. Who else is coming?"

"Just Wang," he told her. "The Europeans haven't finished repairs after the *Copernicus* crash, you know. We offered to carry Duclos or whoever for them, but they declined. I suspect they've about decided to save their money and use secondhand material. The Russians—um—they informed Center that Serov is ill and no substitute immediately available, therefore they'll sit this dance out. My guess is they're hurting more from their last fiscal crisis than they care to admit."

"Wang and me? Well . . . at least we'll be less crowded."

Almeida studied her. She was a tall woman, slender, verging on thinness, though ordinarily her careful dressing and grooming brought a number of excellent features to notice. Her face was likewise rather long and thin: high cheekbones, curved nose, pointed chin, a structure attractive in its way and brought alive by the full mouth, the lustrous dark eyes under arching brows, a complexion to which no one of her age, thirty, had a legal right. The coverall and the normally shoulder-length black hair drawn into a severe bun did her less than justice.

"I didn't realize Wang annoyed you," the intelligence officer said slowly.

She laughed. "On camera the whole time, who makes a pass at whom? Besides, he's robotically correct." Seriously, a touch hesitantly: "No, nothing to complain about. I shouldn't have spoken. He's simply not cheerful company. Under that stiff surface he's too tense, or should I say intense? You feel he never stops watching you, calculating what you'll do next. It gets on the nerves."

Almeida refrained from answering that she had given him an exaggerated description of his impression of her own personality. Her standoffishness, her half-fanatical concentration on work at hand, made him wonder if she had anyone you might call a close friend. . . . Parents and other kin back east, Berdt, Jewish name, didn't that suggest she had a warm place to fly back to? Or had Professor and Mrs. Berdt taken overmuch pride in their brilliant girl, unwittingly driving her from them by urging her without pause toward achievement? . . . Almeida doubted Yvonne had had any bed partner in life except her husband, and that marriage disintegrated within five years . . . two years ago, right? . . . She'd joined the Sigman project shortly before.

He recalled his attention to her: "No worries, Andy. I'll be too busy to notice, this time."

"What? You have a lead?"

"Maybe. A thought that came to me after the last session. I've been working with it since, and a pattern does finally seem to be emerging." Enthusiasm made her suddenly beautiful. But she closed her lips and shook her head. "I'd prefer to say no more until I've tried the idea out."

Almeida tugged his military Vandyke beard. "You've noted it, haven't you, in case of, um, accidents?"

"Certainly. In my study at home, with the rest of my papers." Yvonne rose. "If we're finished here, I'd like a bite to eat."

She couldn't imagine she would ever weary of the sight as her pilot maneuvered toward rendezvous.

In the left window, ten degrees wide at 75,000 kilometers' remove, Earth glowed against the dark. Dayside was a hundred rich shades of blue, swirled over by dazzling pure whitenesses that were weather. The blurred greenish-brown glimpses of land were unidentifiable by her, as if she had already left for shores never trodden. Nightside was black, overlaid with faint shimmers, dancing with brief sparks that might be thunderstorms or might be cities.

Turning her glance away and letting pupils expand after that lambence, she found stars. Because of cabin illumination, they were actually no more than you might see from Pike's Peak, but unwinking and wintry-sharp. Athwart them floated the ship they had sent.

What you saw there was likewise fragmentary. The craft was—perhaps—more an interplay of enigmatic huge forcefields than it was metal, crystal, and synthetic. You saw two spheroids, shining coppery in color. The larger, some hundred meters across, was entirely enclosed. From the hull protruded turrets, needles, discs, frames, domes, webs, less namable objects, at whose functions you could merely guess. They made no ugly chaos. Instead, the shapes and masses had a flowing, breathtaking unity, never static because the eye kept finding new angles, the mind new aspects; Parthenon, Chartres Cathedral, Taj Mahal, Taliesin West could not match this intricate simplicity, this serene dynamism.

About two kilometers aft, locked in place by hydromagnetics (?), a smaller, less spectacularly equipped globe was of skeletal construction, open to the void. Telescopes revealed a pattern which Yvonne couldn't help thinking had charm, playfulness. Yet around it could burn the energies that shape suns. Astronomers had picked out the monstrous blaze of the ship, as it decelerated toward the Solar System, a light-year away. For a year and three-quarters that running star had waxed, while perplexity and anxiety on Earth bred panic often exploding into riot. Yvonne remembered anew how the calm words of Sigurdsen's famous television lecture had turned her own tension to hope, yes, exuberance.

"—beyond doubt a spaceship from another planetary system. R. W. Bussard suggested back in the last century the principle it must be using. Interstellar space is not a total vacuum. In this galactic neighborhood, the gas amounts to about one hydrogen atom per cubic centimeter. Little indeed! However, when you travel at speeds comparable to light's—light speed, the never-quite-reachable maximum which the laws of relativity phsyics permit—when you travel that fast, those few atoms, colliding with your ship, will release X rays and charged particles in such lethal concentration that no material shielding can protect you from nearly instant death.

"No *material* shielding. But we have learned something ourselves about electromagnetic and nuclear forces. The reactor which probably supplies the electricity for your home uses those forces to contain a plasma of hydrogen atoms which move so violently that they fuse to make helium and thus generate power. Bussard theorized that similar forces, on a vast scale, might someday deflect interstellar gas at a safe distance from a starship. He went on to propose that, since the gas was under control, it could be channeled aft, could be made to undergo, it reactions and thereby power the ship. In other words, a Bussard vessel would 'live off the country.' Needing only a modest amount of fuel to get up to ramjet velocity, it could thereafter approach indefinitely close to the ultimate speed. So we could reach the nearer stars, not in millennia but in a mere few years. The gates of the universe would swing wide for humanity.

"Well, we've been anticipated by a more advanced civilization. That body has to be a Bussard-type vessel. No reasonable alternative explanation has been suggested, among the hundreds that have been made. It is a space-craft, coming in at about one-third gravity negative accel-eration, which hints that the crew hails from a smaller planet than Earth. The chances are it comes from a nearby system, quite likely to investigate the curious radio emissions its builders have been detecting from us for the past century. If so, judging by its present course, the most plausible origin is Sigma Draconis. This is a star not unlike Sol, a little more than eighteen light-years distant. We shall see.

"We shall have nothing to fear. On the contrary, we have a cosmos to gain. I know a few of my colleagues worry about the ship's photon drive. Apparently it does not expel matter for thrust. It does still another thing we have not learned how to do. It uses an enormous gas laser to project radiation, a beam of photons, the most efficient kind of reaction motor we can imagine. If a beam of that intensity struck any part of Earth, the devastation would be beyond our imagining.

"*This will not happen.* I agree with those who hold that star-exploring civilizations must be peaceful, because oth-erwise they would have destroyed themselves before reaching the required level of technology. We ourselves, primitive though we are, have been forced—slowly, reluc-tantly, but forced by stark necessity—to create a measure of international stability, international arms control. I do not believe we will fall back into the nightmare condition of nuclear rockets ready to fire. I believe our children and grandchildren will go beyond today's uneasy, often surly limited cooperation, toward positive benignity.

"However, we don't need faith to reassure us about our visitors. They may not be saints, but they cannot be idiots. The least of interstellar distances is an immensity we can denumerate but can never conceive. That is no fleet ap-proaching us, it is a solitary ship—by all indications, smaller than many of ours. Nonetheless it represents an achievement and an investment to beggar the Pyramids, the Great Wall, and the exploration of the Solar System.

What can its crew gain by harming us? What loot can be worth a fraction of the freight charges, what population pressures can be relieved an iota, what ego gratification lies in attacking the defenseless after one has conquered the chasm?

"No, those travelers can only have a single prime desire—knowledge. Adventure and glory too, perhaps, but surely knowledge. And there, I trust, we are not hopelessly outclassed. We have information about entire worlds, planetography, biology, history, anthropology, everything we are and have been, to trade for what they can reveal to us.

"In fact, to be honest, what puzzles me is why the ship has come at all. It would be enormously easier and cheaper to exchange information by laser beams or the like. Obviously the builders of the vessel could have punched a signal here which would attract our notice.

"Are they too impatient for knowledge? It would take many lifetimes to establish a satisfactory mutual language, when thirty-six years must pass between question asked and answer received. A preliminary in-the-flesh expedition could lay the groundwork far more quickly. Thereafter we could indeed use interstellar television. Maybe the Sigma Draconians, if that is their home, have just this one craft, their ambassador to star after star.

"That's merely a guess, of course. I can't wait to learn the truth! Meanwhile, be assured our visitors will take due precautions. They will shut off their dangerous photon engine at the fringes of the Solar System and come in on a suitable drive—probably, I think, a superior version of our ion jet. And they will come in the same peace as the angels came to Bethlehem.

"Children of man, make ready for your guests."

He was right about the alien's harmlessness. But everything else—! And I've since wondered about the harmlessness. What has the cruel, cruel disappointment done to our poor, already sick and divided race? Eagerness returned. *Will I, I, here and now, really find the beginning of the way to lift it?*

"Steady. . . . Roll three degrees. . . . Twelve gauss, wow, let's pull off a ways. . . . Raise thrust six newtons. . . . Bearing ten, zero, two and a half; range eight-point-four. . . . Cut."

Silence, free falling, stars in the windows.

The pilot yawned and stretched. "Okay, Dr. Canter,

here's your stop," he said prosaically. "Want to rest awhile?"

"No, thank you." She shivered. "At once." A second later she remembered to add, "Please."

The copilot nodded. "I'll take you." He unbuckled together with her. Already spacesuited, they made their final checks, secured jetpacks on shoulders, closed helmets, and cycled out the airlock.

Yvonne wished briefly she could cross alone to the ship, amidst the now undimmed splendor of the stars. But no. While her training after she joined the project was intensive, it had not equipped her to meet an emergency in raw space. Linked by a cord to the man's ankles, she hung onto her box of food and other supplies and let him tow her. He went slowly, cautiously, constantly taking sights with his dromometer, to keep them in the tunnel that the Sigman had, for a time, opened in the forces around the vessel. Nevertheless, the humans brushed these more than once. It felt like pulling through a swift current of hot water. Deeper in, at full intensity, an invader would doubtless have been torn apart.

At the shivering translucent curtain of . . . different energies . . . which covered a portal that had dilated in the hull, they stopped. The copilot unsnapped the lifeline from her suit, his free hand keeping a grip on her. Earthlight, reflected off his helmet, made him faceless, and a seething of static distorted his radio voice, as they hung for a moment there between stars and argosy. "Okay?" he asked.

"Yes."

"We'll—don't forget, we'll trail you in orbit. When you're ready to leave, when he dismisses you and flashes the signal, we'll haul around to the present configuration. Wait here for me to come escort you back."

"I'm not as new to these assignments as you seem to be!" she rapped. Recognizing her discourtesy, she made herself add, "No offense meant. Excuse me. I want to get right to work. An extra minute could be precious."

"Sure." He released her. She tapped a control and jetted forward, through the curtain that let her pass but not the ship's air, inboard to confront the Sigman.

III

———◆———

Though he burned to be off with the word that had come to him, Skip finished the mural as promised. His categorical imperative was: "Always leave a clean camp." Urania and the boys kept dropping wistful hints about his staying longer, and they cried when he said goodbye. He didn't take it too hard, especially since his feet would soon have gotten itchy regardless. "I'll try to come back," he said. Maybe he would at that.

A man bound into town for supplies gave him a lift. "Town" was a dozen houses, a couple of stores, a charging station, and a bar. Skip made a dive for the last of these. They only used intoxicants for religious purposes in We. After he came up, snorting and blowing, he put questions to the proprietor. Over his second beer he did some travel arithmetic.

Normally he would have hitchhiked. They still had elbow room in these parts, and thus less reason to be wary of their fellow men than most of Earth's poor rat-frenetic seven-plus billion. He'd have talked with them, asked about things, stopped at wherever looked interesting, often on impulse changed his whole destination. But now he was in a hurry. We's multiplex Lord knew when the Sigman would get tired and leave, and it'd take Skip a while to reach the President of the United States or the High Commissioner of the Peace Authority or whoever else turned out to be appropriate.

Let's count the jingle again. Urania hadn't paid much. There was hardly more personal money per capita in We than in the average sigaroon junction. He hadn't cared, then. Adding the sum to what was in his pockets on arrival—*Damn, that C-coin's in old dollars; divide by a thousand and get a dime*—he reached a total of $233.50. And he must buy food and drink as well as tickets, and these two brews had already set him back four bucks. . . .

22

Call Berkeley? Ask Dad to transfer a bit of credit? He'd be glad to oblige. Skip grimaced. *No.* He hated indebtedness, and the moral part he could never pay, since he had no intention of going george.

He decided to invest in a retrieval. The public phone was about the only modern item in the pleasant, cool and dim archaism of the tavern: so up-to-date that it didn't take coins. If Skip had put his credit card in the slot, the No Funds bulb would have kindled in its unnecessarily snotty fashion. He borrowed the proprietor's, after showing he had cash to cover charges. The phone screen lit with a recording, a pretty girl whose smile was probably just as automatic in the flesh. "Data service. May we help you?"

He punched out essential words on the keyboard to avoid bringing in an expensive live operator. Elsewhere on the continent, a computer routed the inquiry to the appropriate memory bank; electron beams scanned giant molecules and drew forth the information contained in their distortions; after a minute's wait—channels must be crowded today—the recording said, "Your answer is ready. Do you wish a printout?"

"No, thanks," Skip said, his natural memory being cheaper. He wondered why he thanked these gadgets. Words unrolled on the screen, slowly until he turned the speed knob.

What Keeper caravans are where? Reply: Morgan's in Connecticut on an erosion contract; the Friends of Earth reforesting in Wisconsin; the Terrans on a rescue mission clear off in Egypt, along with several similar outfits from other countries, under aegis of the Environment Authority; Commonweal doing flood control in Alabama—

When the screen blanked, Skip paid the proprietor and returned to his beer and calculations. He'd worked for the Terrans last year, was well thought of among them, had hoped their chief would give him his first boost toward his goal. But he'd not make it to Egypt on the wing in any reasonable time, and he'd have the problem of getting back. *Besides, I don't want to go. News pictures are as much as I can take of what happens when the ecology of an overpeopled land collapses.* The Tuatha de Danaan were nearest, at Lake Tahoe, but who was he to them? He'd have to enroll in their auxiliaries and spend six months proving himself before he could likely get a recommendation to someone really influential.

No, wait. He'd followed the Tahoe job with interest. It

involved more than restoring purity of waters and the wilderness around them. It covered that whole part of the Sierra. Besides watershed, wildlife, timber, and recreation, agriculture was in the plans. Carefully located farms, crops and techniques lately developed for uplands, would not simply throw a little extra food into the world's ever hungrier gape. They could make a positive contribution toward maintaining nature's balance, and the owners could double as wardens. Small, isolated, such a spread was made to order for a Freeman—and the government had promised homesteading rights to qualified persons who worked for the duration of the project—and the nearest Freemen to Tahoe were those in Mendocino County, who were Skip's friends—

"Hey, bartender, you know if anybody's driving north today?"

The bus was crowded. Most things were, around population centers. Mosiah hadn't lasted long as a shiny decent-sized New Town; the Salt Lake City-Provo octopus engulfed it. This ride being express, straight through to Reno, Skip had no great hope of shaking the bore who had settled next to him.

"—barbarism," said the gray man. "Not decadence, barbarism. You're an example, if you'll pardon me. Not your fault. A factory turned you out, not a school, most certainly not a college. And why?" He tapped his seatmate's knee. "Because nobody cares. No respect for learning, scholarship, humanities; hardly any surviving awareness that such phenomena ever existed."

Skip sighed and looked out the window. The bus boomed over a land once again blessedly empty. Through dust kicked up by the air-cushion drive, Skip saw alkali-white ground thinly strewn with sagebrush, distant bluish-brown mountains, a couple of buzzards wheeling far aloft. He wished the window could be opened or at least weren't self-darkening—hot pungent air, incandescent sunlight. ... A contrail crossed heaven, and another and another. He wished he could afford a first-class jet. Or a jumbo—no less a cattle car than this, but it would liberate him faster.

"You haven't been educated, you've been processed," said the gray man.

Skip debated whether to show him the paperback of Robinson Jeffers in his tunic pocket. No, that might encourage him. *Well, shall I slap him in the face with the truth? Something like:*

—My parents, sir, explained the situation to me, I believe correctly. They are intelligent, open-minded people who give thought to what they experience. I differ from them but that does not diminish my respect for their brains.

—As children they witnessed the last fashionable radicalism and youthism. For years thereafter they heard aging members of the Now Generation lament how the ungrateful young rejected the wisdom of their elders. My parents' own generation, however, was too busy surviving for capitalized Causes: too busy surviving intellectually, sometimes physically, in schools more packed, more explosively mixed, for each year that passed. Sir, how could the children of the poor at first, but presently the children of all except the very rich, be taught anything, unless a fresh look was taken at the problem, unless every philosopher of education from Plato to Skinner was called into scientific question, unless an engineering approach threw overboard that metaphor misnamed "psychology" and applied the findings of rigorous research on man as a whole organism?

—The teaching machine was a mere beginning. Psychophysiological conditioning followed. Subliminal exposure was the aspect that roused most controversy, but simpler and subtler approaches went deeper. For instance, after it was found what is the most effective kind of positive reinforcement—reward, if you choose—for a child's giving the right response, the rate of learning and retention skyrocketed.

—Yes, indeed, most education today, clear through college, is just another technology. And I am glad. It has saved me years of ennui, out of these too few that I was granted.

—Your problem, sir, is that you were born too late. You are a professor in an era when academe is no longer taken seriously. The researchers have been lured away by industry and government. The rare, genuine, born teacher necessarily restricts the number of his disciples. You have the title, you are equipped with a full battery of platitudes, but none except a pathetic handful like yourself pay attention. In the public mind, educators have been relegated to the skilled-technician class, along with repairmen, police officers, doctors, astronauts—

No. That would be too cruel. Skip contented himself with saying, "Don't ask me. I'm only a vagabond."

"You've given up the struggle, then."

Skip shrugged. "What's to struggle for?"

The professor pinched his lips together. "The sense of drift, as Toynbee wrote. Why strive, when the current sweeps us helpless toward the brink?" He leaned close. The abrupt intensity of his stare and his tone astounded Skip. "We might have coped with the machine," he declared. "We might have hoped for a renaissance after the dark age descending on us. But not when that devil's ship pollutes our sky."

"Huh?"

"The alien. The Sigman. The thing from outside. Don't you see, however inhuman, a machine is nevertheless a product of humanity? But this being, this monster ... obscenely hideous, its very body a jeer at man ... the incalculable power, the arrogance of Satan—no, worse than that, for Satan is at least a human archetype—and we make a god of it, in some instances literally—we rack our best brains, we spend billions of dollars that could feed starving children—on Moloch, on trying to twist ourselves into so inhuman a way of thinking that we can converse with Moloch in his own language and semantics!"

The professor drew breath. He leaned back and said more levelly: "Oh, I know the arguments about the Sigman's peacefulness. I'm not convinced. Still they might be correct. Don't you see, though, it doesn't matter? The Sigman is the epitome of the final dehumanization. Whether we die or become slaves or flesh-and-blood robots or two-legged caricatures of Sigmans, makes no difference. *Man will be gone from the universe.*"

"What do you suggest?" Skip ventured. "We should ignore that ship till the pilot quits and goes home?"

"We should destroy it," said the professor, and now he spoke quite calmly. "I would be proud, no, joyful to smuggle an atomic bomb aboard and detonate it."

Frustration breeds fanatics, Skip decided.

It came to him that he'd heard more paranoia about the ship than you might expect, especially from low-rank members of the Ortho like this fellow. The remarks had made no special impression on him, since he generally avoided extended conversations with persons he found dreary. And what was drearier than the class which his seatmate typified?

They didn't have the talent to become high-paid managers, engineers, scientists, politicians, any of the professionals who, with spit and baling wire, kept civilization somehow creaking along. Nor could they become the equally expensive entertainers who lubricated the machine. They were routineers, who rarely had much to offer that a computer-effector hookup couldn't supply better.

No doubt morality as well as timidity kept them from dropping down to the Underworld. But lack of originality as well as lack of nerve restrained them from joining any Byworld subculture, let alone starting a new one. In a pathetic and, te Skip, fairly horrible manner, these shopkeepers, clerks, office flunkies, holders of titles that the real Ortho hadn't gotten around to abolishing, continued to ape their masters and tell themselves that they too were essential.

The wonder was that hatreds did not ferment in more of their brains. Public opinion polls said a large majority of Americans were pro-Sigman.

Hm. How reliable are the polls, in a country as kaleidoscopic as this'n's become? And what about foreign countries? And how many minds have changed, after three years of negative? And what demagogue might find here the exact issue he needs?

Yes, I'd better hustle.

Currently the Tuatha de Danaan were on the south shore of Lake Tahoe, which most urgently needed them. The hordes who had defeated every earlier attempt at rehabilitation were gone. The resorts and clip joints which drew them had been razed, after the inmates had been redistributed in various New Towns. Condemnation proceedings never had been much of a political hurdle since California's Central Valley turned into malodorous desert. Nor was new topsoil hard to come by, what with container dumps bio-degrading everywhere you went. But the soil must be distributed, fertilized, watered, planted to the right species. When that first, quick-growing lot of trees and bushes had made a forest of sorts, the first kinds of wildlife must be introduced. Meanwhile you worked your way around the banks. And processing the entire lake, to get rid of contaminants and algae, would take years.

The camp didn't welcome tourists, but applications for employment were solicited. Skip told a guard jokes for an hour and won a pass to "look around and see if I might fit in." Two more hours of sauntering, gabbing, and inquiring led him to Roger Neal, whom he'd known in Mendocino.

The younger-son Freeman was working for an eventual hearth and home-acre of his own. His assignment was to a less pastoral scene than close to the fence, where trees remained and a few entomological technicians were stocking bugs that attacked plant pests. Here, on a steep red slope, bulldozers rumbled, dirtspreaders upchucked, graders whuffled, a hundred men swarmed and shouted above the noise. Most of that racket came from the water, where it roared down the tubes of barge-mounted processors and spouted back, white under a brilliant sun. Yet locally the lake was glittering again, jewel blue; and kilometers away, scars hidden by distance, peaks held forth a promise of what might someday come back.

Might, Skip had thought. *I dunno. India, Egypt, half China . . . oh, huge chunks of this planet—Who says North America hasn't already gone too far down that same road? If some of us, a few of us, could start fresh on a new world—*

Roger, muscular, sunburned, his work clothes muddied, shook hands vigorously. "Great to see you! Gonna sign on? 'Fraid we can't have another Night of the Barn—no girls here—but a weekend in Hangtown, these days, is something to remember. What you been doing, horn? Bet you got a million yarns to spin. Bet four of 'em are true."

Skip grinned. He had first met Rog when, at fifteen, his chronic restlessness led him to a summer job on that farm. He had found the Freemen pretty straitlaced. They were, in fact, still another utopian movement, attempting to restore the independent, patriarchal yeoman on a basis of modern agronomics, cheap and sophisticated equipment, abundant power, easy electronic communication with the outside world. The Night of the Barn had called on Skip's full resources of generalship and deviousness to arrange. None of the adults having ever learned about it, he remained welcome among the Mendocino colonists and could always pick up a little jingle odd-jobbing for them.

"Five," he said. "You forgot the normal kind. What do you mean, no girls? Wild, glamorous Keeper women—where's your initiative?"

"Too big a ration of auxiliaries to cadre, this project. Too much competition. Hangtown's easier. I will say, though, on fiesta nights, watching those alices dance amongst the fires—yeah, I'll stay in camp for that."

Skip nodded, recalling his time among the Terrans. Keepers, full-time conservers and restorers, might live in mobile houses of necessity; a man on a task of months or years would want his family around, and kids could get their formal education via multiple-hookup two-way screens. The nomad communities might thus become close-knit; they might come to view what they did romantically, almost religiously, as the most important work on Earth; they would develop their special folkways; yes, all quite natural. But Skip suspected that the gypsylike overtones, the holidays where ceremony and conviviality flowed together, the plangent songs, the colorful garb ... had their growth not been forced a wee bit? An extra inducement for outside help?

No matter. He'd enjoyed himself.

"I'm not after a billet, Rog," he said. "I'd like to talk with you when you get off."

"Sure. Spend the night. The food's okay. I'll sign a chit for you. You can spread your sack on my bunkhouse floor, or on the ground if you prefer. My mates'll be delighted."

Skip made himself unobtrusive till the 5:30 whistle blew. The Keepers' help had no objections to a forty-hour week. Overtime pay was welcome when there wasn't much to do in camp but earn it.

He explained his errand. Rog didn't have immediate access to Chief Keough, but his foreman did. Skip spent the evening winning over the foreman, which wasn't hard. The fellow was fresh from Alaska, where you rarely met a sigaroon, so to him the song-jape-story routine was enchanting. He gladly made an appointment on Skip's behalf "to talk about an idea that might be useful."

Daniel Keough, next noon, was a different case. He'd seen hundreds like his visitor. His courtesy was gruff. "Sit yourself, Mr. Wayburn. I'm afraid I can't spare you a lot of time."

Skip eased into a folding chair, like the one which held Keough's huge frame. Working or no, the chief wore fringed pants, embroidered tunic, red sash and beret, silver on neck and wrists. His wife and daughters, flitting in and out of the dirigible dwelling, were still more gaudy. The latter cast glances at Skip which made him wish he could stay. Around, pines climbed green into blue heaven. A butterfly cruised through sun-speckled sweet-smelling shadows, a bird whistled, a squirrel ran fiery up a bole. Distantly came the noise of the machines that sought to bring this back everywhere.

"Reckon I'll have to convince you fast, sir."

Keough puffed his pipe and waited.

"I want to see President Braverman," Skip said. "Or

Commissioner Uchida or somebody like that, somebody at the top of the office."

Keough's brows lifted in the seamed, bronzed face. "How can I help you?"

"By passing me on to the right person, sir. You see, I doubt if anybody in this country is more than, oh, ten steps away from the top. Usually fewer. Like, I know my father, who knows a state committeeman of the Popular Party, who must be buddy-buddy with our Senators, who've got the ear of the President. Like that."

Keough stroked his beard. "Then' why not ask your father?"

"I may. But only for backup, an extra smidgin of influence. Politicians will tend to dismiss me as a crank, and they've learned how to slough off cranks—Darwinian necessity." Keough chuckled, which encouraged Skip to continue. Nonetheless he felt nervous enough that, hardly thinking about it, he took pad and pencil from his tunic and started sketching while he spoke. "They will listen to a reputable scientist or engineer. And that kind is likelier to listen to me. And you, sir, must know any number of such. Please help. It's urgent. Not for me. I don't care who delivers my message, if he delivers it straight. This is for the human race."

Keough's eyes veiled.

"I know," Skip said. "A beardless boy intends to save the world. Aren't cranks generally older? All I want to do is give the authorities an idea that doesn't seem to have hit them. If I wrote to Washington, you know I'd get a form letter thanking me for my interest in democracy. But if you tell somebody respected, who respects you, that you think I may be on to something, he'll listen. And so it'll go."

"What's that you're doodling?" Keough asked sharply.

"Huh? Oh . . . nothing. I guess what you're doing here suggested it." Skip passed the cartoon over. A few lines showed a steppe, in the background a burning town, in the foreground several mounted Mongols of Genghis Khan's time. They were looking in some dismay at a leader who, pointing furiously to a lone blade of grass, exclaimed, "Who's responsible for this?"

Skip didn't think the little jest rated such volcanic laughter. "Okay," Keough said. "You've earned yourself five minutes."

At the end of them, he said, "Go on."

After an hour, he sprang to his feet. "You could be flat

wrong," he roared, "but what's to lose? And a galaxy to grab! Sure, I'll buck you on, lad. I'll arrange your transportation, too. If you are wrong, if you never do another deed in your life worth a belch, remember, you did give old Dan Keough an hour's hope for his grandchildren!"

IV

———◆———

Beyond the energy curtain was a short tubular passage set with odd projections that might be handgrips. Yvonne used them to pull herself along. The corridor, like the room to which it led, was lined with an unknown material, smooth, slightly yielding, in which colors swirled and eddied, a slow, intricate dance that could fascinate you close to hypnotism if you watched. The substance also provided adequate neutral illumination.

From the passage Yvonne entered a hemispherical chamber, about thirty meters in radius. It likewise was provided with grips, whereon successive human visitors had secured sleeping harness, cameras, portable analytical kits, and other such gear, until its original harmony was lost in clutter. A paraboloid bulged into it, leaving a maximum of four meters between sections.

This seemed to be a verandah projecting from whatever rooms lay behind. It was transparent, seemingly unbroken. On occasion it had dilated, when the Sigman passed out small biological samples in glass containers through a one-way force screen. The being had declined the terrestrial specimens offered, by simply not admitting them, and had made no further presents since the early days.

The light within the dome was orange-yellow in hue and more intense than what falls on Earth. The atmosphere likewise differed from the kind provided in the "guest quarters." The Sigman had obliged with a bottleful. The composition turned out to be approximately like Earth's on a humid day, but twice as dense. Bolometers indicated a tropical temperature, variable but averaging 33° C. How these facts could be reconciled with the hypothesis that the planet of origin was smaller than man's, no one was sure and everyone wanted greatly to know.

It was likewise unclear why the dome was crowded, not only with a three-dimensional lattice of fixed objects

(mostly adjustable, frequently moving or changing shape
as if of themselves, none understandable to men albeit
always pleasing to the eye) but with a hundred varieties, a
thousand colors of plants (blue-green fronded leaves, ex-
quisite when they weren't magnificent) which seemingly
grew out of certain lattice members. To renew oxygen?
But man already had more efficient methods for that.
Some unheard-of symbiosis? A hobby, to relieve loneliness? An aspect of religion? Scientists had come to damn
their beauty. It blocked them from seeing more than a
few meters past the inner wall.

The Sigman rarely showed itself before its visitors had
unsuited and stowed their baggage. Yvonne did this quickly. She had soon gotten the hang of operating in weightlessness. Bluestocking she might be, but she was in addition a good swimmer and ferocious tennis player.

The air was comfortably warm. It held a slight spicy
odor. The utter stillness—ventilation without pumps was
another trick humans would like to acquire—added to the
surreal feeling of flight. Yvonne suppressed a desire to
indulge in acrobatics as sternly as she suppressed the wish
for a cigarette. A job was on hand. She checked the
cameras and recording instruments, which had naturally
been left going. Ample tape remained. Doubtless it held as
little of interest as all its predecesors.

*Blast it, the Sigman can't be busy every moment on
those junkets around our system! This ship must be wholly
self-running; ours almost are. I can imagine the creature
taking off to make planetological studies or simply to
break the monotony. I can even see that it might not care
to have us around for more than limited periods of time.
But why won't it go on camera and start establishing a
language? Point to a drawing or photograph or whatever
of something, make a noise or write a word. Lord knows
our people tried. They'd point to a companion and say,
"Man." They'd diagram the Solar System, the periodic
table, the water molecule. We never got a response in
kind.*

*I think the suggestion must be right, that the Sigman
refuses our specimens because it already knows about
them. Perhaps they are dangerous to it. (Though we,
taking elaborate precautions, found nothing to fear. How
could a life using dextro amino acids and levo sugars eat
us, let alone infect us?) More plausible is the idea that this
is not the first Sigman visit. A long development must lie
behind a ship as perfected as this; and Sol is among their*

nearer stars. Probably they made their scientific studies ten thousand years ago. Or one thousand; we'd have no reliable record. Probably Earth's radio emission attracted them back and our visitor is a cultural anthropologist.

Then why doesn't it act like one?

And if, contrariwise, it has no interest in us, why does it admit us at all?

The thoughts, worn smooth by repetition, passed through Yvonne's head like a tune she couldn't shake loose. She must concentrate too hard on her chores. But when, at last, she had placed her cluster of apparatus on the dome with suction cups, and herself in an aluminum frame similarly fastened—then her new thoughts rushed forth, and she quivered with eagerness.

The Sigman came.

No amount of earnest effort could altogether prevent the sight from turning her slightly queasy. Many people, seeing it on television, were physically sickened. "We look as horrible to it as it does to us" had become a cliché, like "This ought to show us how tiny the differences between humans really are." Neither had made many converts.

A comedian had described the being as a cross between a slug and a pinecone. The phrase stuck. About three meters long, 130 centimeters thick, the body was a flexible ellipsoid shingled in squarish golden-brown plates. Those were independently mounted, on muscular stalks at three different levels, so that seen from outside they overlapped. When the Sigman stretched itself, cameras occasionally recorded glimpses of the inner body thus protected, a spongy black mass.

Symmetry was preserved by four stumpy, shell-covered legs near the middle, with disc-shaped webbed feet, and by a pair of arms farther out at either end. Hence the Sigman had no front or rear; it moved and worked as easily "backward" as "forward." Each arm possessed shoulder joint, elbow, and wrist, but there the resemblance to man's stopped. The hard brown material sheathed it like a crab's. Vaguely crustacean, too, were the four mandibles at the end, whose cutting and grinding surfaces worked against each other. The Sigman had been observed eating. The claws macerated what must be food, then held the mess against the spongy surface they surrounded. There, apparently, fierce digestive juices broke it down till it was absorbed straight up the arms.

The claws in turn were, set by set, surrounded by six

ropy short tentacles. These made excellent fingers but, to a man, suggested a snakepit.

Retractible beneath the shingles or extensible between them, here and there over the whole body, were assorted thin tendrils. Presumably they were sensors but, aside from four unmistakable eyes, their functions remained unidentified.

The plates always glistened, not simply with moisture but with dripping slimes that were thought to be excreted matter.

Yvonne had her repugnance well under control. "Hello," she said. Her smile, she knew, was useless.

The shape hauled itself through the lattice until two of those stalked, unwinking black eyes stared into hers. Fog wraiths curled behind; water droplets formed on leaves, broke loose and danced among them like tiny stars.

The Sigman boomed. Somehow sound was passed through the dome. Phonograms were automatically made. Yvonne wondered how many thousand man-hours had been spent poring over them. She'd contributed plenty herself.

Before her was a console from which a wire ran back to the sonic synthesizer that had been installed. It could reproduce elements of Sigman speech, if speech was what those noises were, in any combination. To date it had gotten no response, had seemed rather to make the Sigman go away sooner.

Yvonne refreshed memory by a glance at her clipboarded notes, and struck the first of the phrases she had planned. It came forth as a chord, twanging bass through treble, simultaneous chirp and whistle.

Will it work? Her heartbeat shook her.

The Sigman's eyestalks rose rigid.

Yvonne played a second phrase. Claws spread wide. The creature was showing more reaction than to any previous attempt. Yvonne let the notes die away. She took from her clipboard the first of a series of photographs and drawings. It showed a nude man. She played the phrase again.

A slight variation in it accompanied the picture of a woman. A third variation was associated with a mixed group. The Sigman extended tendril after tendril. Was it getting the idea at last? Did it realize that she was suggesting words for "human-male," "human-female," "humans"?

The Sigman trilled and withdrew from sight. Yvonne waited, head awhirl. The Sigman returned quickly, carrying a small globular object. *The projector!* flashed through Yvonne. *O God, O God, it hasn't brought that out for more than two years!*

In the air appeared a three-dimensional multicolored interweaving of shapes, curves, lines. It flowed through changes, complex and beautiful as running water. The Sigman meanwhile piped and growled, waved tendrils in a kind of ballet, and exuded a fine spray of yellow fluid.

Yvonne shook her head. Disappointment was like a belly blow. "I don't understand," she said, dry-mouthed.

The Sigman paused. Silence waxed. And then, retracting most of its tendrils, it operated to project a red band whose pointed end was directed at itself. It waited. She brought forth a chord. The Sigman repeated it. The band swung to indicate her. She sounded what she had given for "woman" and heard it given back.

For a second, darkness passed through her. She came out of the near faint sobbing, but for glory. After three years, the stranger was ready to help create a common language.

Yvonne turned when her teammate's spacesuited form floated in. *Damn!* was her first reaction. In the flame of achievement, she had actually forgotten Wang Li was due to join her. Then she realized she was atremble with tension and the sweat that soaked her coverall gave off an unladylike smell.

Maybe the Sigman welcomed a break too. It stuck the optical projecter between two bars which lifted from the deck in superb helices, and floated off into the flowers. Presently leaves began to wave and rustle; it had turned a blower on them, as it often did.

Yvonne paused not to wonder why. With jittering fingers she assembled her notes. She went to the sound recorder and tapped its keys, projecting onto the screen the successive phonograms of the words.

"Good day, Dr. Canter."

Her exasperation vanished. She couldn't help herself, even before this man she didn't like. He had unsuited and now hung close beside her, lightly holding a handgrip. Her arms went around him, almost knocking him loose. She cried into his ear: "I've done it! We've won! We have the key!"

"What?" His habitual impassivity broke to the extent of widened eyes and open mouth. "Are you certain?"

She released him. "Ten words, this past hour," she

chattered. "We ran through them over and over, m-m-making sure there was no mistake. See, no, listen, I'll play back the tapes, you can look at my notes and the 'grams—here, pictures of several different men, color, clothes, build ... the Sigman itself can't confuse them ... and I got the same word each time, 'human-male'—" The clipboard slipped from her grasp and twirled out of reach.

Wang retrieved it. He stayed where he was, paging through the sheets, frowning in his concentration. *Maybe just as well he's such a cold fish,* Yvonne thought while she calmed down. *If he were somebody who could celebrate, I might ... have done anything. And we do have a long, tough haul before us, calling for every brain cell we've got.*

She studied him. He was a North Chinese, hence taller than she though of slender build. Clean-shaven in the manner of his country, his face was strong in jaws and nose, beneath a high forehead and short gray hair. Free fall or no, he remained ramrod-straight in the drab brown quasi-uniform common among officials of the People's Republic. For he was not simply a professor at Peking University. The government had backed his research into what was called "linguatherapy" more because the results might help in absorbing Tibetans, Mongols, and other minorities, than for their possible value in treating mental illness. (She did assume that he himself had had the latter purpose in mind.)

"Wonderful, if true," he said at length. His English was fluent, the accent slight. "No discourtesy, of course. But we have had false hopes in the past. The Sigman would apparently be cooperative, but after minutes it would go away for hours, and has invariably dismissed us within a few days."

"Exactly," Yvonne answered. "I've had a full hour. And for the first time, as I said, the results are reproducible. It will adopt any word I give it in association with something, and repeat that word next time the something is indicated. Always before, it seemed to be trying to teach us a word of its own, but disappeared very shortly when we played those phonemes back. And our attempts at setting up vocal or visual codes had still more dismal endings. I tell you, now— Wait! It's returning! You'll see for yourself."

The Sigman carried an iridescent ovoid, which it attached to a bar near the dome wall. "I have seen that thing," Wang said, "albeit not for some while. I believe it is a recording device."

"Sure. It'd about given up on trying to comunicate with us. But now that we can build a mutual language, naturally it'll have to take notes."

Yvonne and the Sigman got back to work. Wang Li floated motionless, watching. The cameras filmed nothing dramatic—exchange of sounds, woman holding up pictures, nonhuman projecting recognizable copies (as a David painting might recognizably have suggested one by Van Gogh)—what was happening was too big for drama.

At the end of two more hours, the Sigman had evidently had enough for a while and retired. Yvonne didn't mind. She felt wrung out. Entering the sanitary cubicle, she undressed, sponged herself clean, and donned a fresh coverall. Emerging, she found that Wang had opened the rations and started them heating at the glower. He already had a squeeze bottle of coffee for her.

"Thanks." It warmed and relaxed her. She strapped her body loosely into place and stretched out.

"A pity we have no champagne," he said, faintly smiling.

"Oh, I seldom drink. I would like a smoke—tobacco, I mean, not marijuana."

"We are similar in that respect." Wang's look was very steady on her. "Would you like to explain your accomplishment? It really does seem as if you have succeeded, and I offer congratulations both heartfelt and humble."

Down underneath, he's human. Maybe that thought joined with triumph and with the need to uncoil, to make her feel friendlier toward him than would otherwise have been the case. And they were, after all, alone in this strange, quiet room.

"Certainly." She sipped. "Only . . . well, I'm tired, my mind's in disarray. May I keep things on a kindergarten level and tell you stuff you know as well as you know your name?"

"That might actually be best. It will give perspective and point out what, in a welter of data, is significant. Your eventual full report may not be easy reading for me."

The words rushed from her as if she were intoxicated:

"Perhaps not. You recall my research before this project was in mathematical semantics, though my Ph.D. was in comparative linguistics. I used a lot of math.

"What was the situation? The Sigman can't produce human-type sounds; its appear to come from a set of vibrating tympani. We can't produce Sigman vocables.

That is, we can with the synthesizer, but it's almost impossibly difficult. Ten fingers, moving through electromagnetic fields, are supposed to generate a high-fidelity version of a language that uses hundreds of frequencies and amplitudes simultaneously?

"Not having a corresponding instrument—and I think, now, I know why not—the Sigman attempted at first to teach men its tongue. Those sounds, those incomprehensible however lovely drawings and whatnot it exhibited ... we didn't get the idea. I mean, none of the research teams did; I wasn't here at the start, of course. We tried showing objects and pictures ourselves. The Sigman would make a noise. We'd take a phonogram of that noise, feed this into the synthesizer, and try haltingly to combine elements to get higher abstractions. 'Man' and 'Sigman' together equals 'intelligent beings'—that sort of thing. The Sigman quickly retreated to its inner suite.

"We guessed its language might be so hopelessly alien that our combinations were nonsensical. In fact, I've always felt Fuentes' idea is right. The Sigman language is only vocal in part. Position, gesture, perhaps odors emitted at will, may be more important. Therefore communication may be extremely subtle and complex. It may be nonlinear, it may involve many concepts at once that we humans put separately, it may deal with whole aspects of reality where we have to take a piece at a time. The cellular study of those biological samples hints at something like this.

"Well, if we couldn't learn Sigman, might the opposite approach work? We tried to build an artificial language from the ground up, one that it could pronounce and we could synthesize and both races could comprehend. The attempt got results just as bad, or worse. Do you realize that in three years men have been aboard this vessel a total of ninety-eight days?"

"I keep track," Wang said. "Ah, I believe dinner is ready."

Yvonne sighed. "I did have a reason for that lecture. Your suggestion that I emphasize the points which spurred my thinking. Or did I need to? Maybe I'm high on happiness."

"Please say whatever you desire." Wang handed her her rack. To simplify work, meals were standardized. "Tonight" they both had fish filet, fried rice and onions (in squeeze bags), bok choy (in covered disposable dishes), and cookies. They scarcely noticed.

"The real job I did can't be put in words," Yvonne said.

"It involved every kind of statistical analysis of data that I could think of. If I didn't have a priority on computer time, I'd still be at it.

"Oh, yes, others have done the same. But none of those people demonstrated that any patterns they found were significant. Remember, given finite sets of numbers, you can construct a literal infinity of functions relating them. I applied some results from my earlier work in human linguistics, especially a theorem I'm quite proud of. That let me make quantitative predictions of the consequences of certain hypotheses which occurred to me."

She stopped to chew. Wang ate on, imperturbably.

"Well, I'll give you the results," Yvonne said. "First, I can show that we've been going too fast. The frequencies with which identifiable combinations recur in the Sigman's utterances average out at half the median of human languages. Maybe it actually thinks more slowly, if more deeply, than we do. But if I'm wrong about this, our comparative machine-gun chatter must at any rate be confusing and annoying. The confusion it could overcome —the annoyance, not. In fact, I suspect we've been inflicting outright pain."

Wang's hand paused halfway to his mouth.

Yvonne nodded. "Your people hear English as harsh and staccato, mine hear Chinese as high-pitched and sing-song," she said. "Not too pleasant till one gets used to it. Our musics are a still more clear-cut example. Actually, I enjoy some Chinese music, as you perhaps enjoy my beloved Beethoven, but to many of my countrymen a concert would be excruciating. We needn't go outside of a single society, though. I find today's popular American music merely banal. But I've heard recordings from, oh, fifty years back. Having to sit through an evening of that stuff would be, to me, literal torture.

"I came to believe the Sigman simply can't endure our clumsy attempts to make its kind of sounds.

"And that, I think, is why it didn't bring a synthesizer. Continuous human speech would have been unbearable. Attempts at communication by visual symbols broke down for similar reasons. Our drawings, our alphabet are too ugly, perhaps too angular. Maybe we should have tried Chinese characters."

Wang frowned while he consumed the interrupted morsel. "Would so shrinkingly sensitive a soul cross interstellar space?" he asked finally.

"We don't know its psychology. Suppose it, trying to speak to us, kept making noises like a fingernail scraping on a blackboard—or else those subsonic notes that induce fear reactions. Many humans couldn't have stood that.

"I admit you have a good point, Professor Wang, so good that no one before me thought it might be invalid. Oh, the question may not turn on actual pain. The trouble may, as I said before, just be annoyance. The Sigman may keep going off in a huff because we keep making such awful cacophonies.

"So I went back to the tapes and phonograms and analyzed them for musical rules."

"Intonation?" Wang asked at once.

Yvonne laughed. "I'm not sure. Principally what I found were relationships like those governing our scales and keys. Furthermore, there are relationships between tonal qualities—some occur together, some don't—and the interludes between them. It's extraordinarily complicated. I doubt if I've extracted more than a fraction yet.

"But I could see what we'd done wrong. We can record a phrase and play it back with high fidelity. However, Sigman grammar doesn't operate by tacking phrases together, any more than a heavily inflected language like Latin does. Besides, the method is hopelessly slow and awkward. Later we tried creating an artificial speech, with the synthesizer making Sigman-type vocables. Only we got every relationship wrong. The effect was as bad—as irritating or outright painful—as that of a tone-deaf person trying to sing. Or worse, probably.

"What I did, therefore, was start fresh. The computer helped me devise a spoken language which obeys the basic harmony rules but which is not too complicated to produce on the synthesizer. And it can't be hopelessly amiss ... because the Sigman *is* working on learning it!"

Wang sat quiet a long while before he nodded. "Wonderful indeed." His smile didn't seem to go further than the teeth. Well, no doubt he felt a degree of jealousy, on his country's behalf if not his own.

"Oh, I anticipate," Yvonne confessed. "This is very new. What I have, thus far, is about a hundred nouns, verbs, and adjectives that can be defined ostensively. I've roughed out a pidgin grammar, the simplest and least ambiguous I could invent on short notice. It's positional, like English or Chinese. So far the only inflections are to show plurals. I think we'll want them for tenses too, but maybe not. Maybe the Sigmans have a time-concept like the Hopi. We'll have to feel our way. But we'll get there!"

The existing vocabulary was soon conveyed, and a few trial sentences constructed. That went less well. Perhaps Sigmans didn't make anything strictly corresponding to sentences. However, toward the end the nonhuman was projecting its eldritch sketches in animation and suiting words to the actions depicted. "Man walks. Men walk. Sigman walks. Men and Sigmans walk. Planet rotates. Planet revolves. Blue planet revolves. Green planet revolves. Blue and green planets rotate and revolve."

Wang watched, studied her notes, made occasional suggestions, generally kept in the background.

On the third day the Sigman dismissed the Earthlings. The indication was a warbling note. After the first two times, when a gradual but inexorable drop in air pressure followed, men had gotten the message.

"I'm not sorry, to be honest," Yvonne said. "I suspect it wants to rest and ponder. And I could use a rest myself."

"You deserve one," Wang replied tonelessly.

Their respective spacecraft removed them in response to a red flicker-signal. Yvonne took the records—films, tapes, plates, rolls, from a score of scientific instruments— because it was an American's turn to do so. The rule impressed her as ridiculous, when they were promptly scanned for the public data banks; but it hung on.

Or is "ridiculous" the proper word? crossed momentarily through her joy. *The arrangement means nothing per se. However, as a symbol of anachronisms that are deadly dangerous in an era when men can blow up the world—I wonder.*

V

———◆———

Behind the desk, which seemed wide and glassy to Wang Li as a fusion bomb crater, General Chou Yuan reared upright in his chair. "You did not even demand immediate transmission of her computations?" he exclaimed.

Wang bent his head. "No, Comrade General," he said miserably. "It . . . did not occur to me. She promised to send the material soon. But it is in her apartment, where she has her study, and . . . no doubt her superiors will keep her on base for a while . . . and journalists, considering what a sensation the news must be—"

"It is that." Chou's tone was grim. His broad face seldom showed much expression, but he was scowling now, and he drummed on the desktop. For Wang, those uniformed shoulders blocked out most of the window behind. Blue summer air of Earth, glimpse of utterly green trees and a soaring arc of temple roof on Prospect Hill, stood infinitely remote. A breeze wandering in had somehow lost freshness, carried nothing save the endless murmur of Peking's traffic.

Despite noise, the office held a stretched silence. And it was bare; except for the tenant—no, with the tenant—how bare and barren! On the right wall hung a portrait of Lenin, on the left one of Mao. Wang felt that their eyes, and the eyes of Chairman Sung's picture at his back, drilled into him.

What am I afraid of? I am a patriot, they know that, they trust me. . . . Public humiliation? No, I must not think of confession and correction before my friends as "humiliation." Have I been too much in the West? Perhaps the Western virus has entered my blood and needs cleaning out— It came to Wang why he trembled. They might take him off the Sigman project, just when it was unfolding like a blossom in springtime.

43

"Catastrophic, this news babbled over the radio on Canter's way down," Chou said. "Could you not have advised discretion until the possibilities for good or ill have been considered?"

"I never dreamed it could be anything but occasion for delight, Comrade General." Inspiration: "Chairman Sung has repeatedly instructed us that an advanced society like our visitor's can only be anti-imperialistic and can only have correct thoughts to offer."

"Yes. Yes." Chou sat still for a moment. "Well, when do you expect to receive Canter's material?"

"Not for days at best, I fear. She told me it was disorganized, considerable of it in her private abbreviations, and she would write a formal report."

"More delay! And if and when the Americans let her transmit to us, publish to the world—will they allow a full and truthful account?"

"Why should they not?" Wang asked, startled half out of his worry.

"Comrade Professor, you have been abroad more than most, have correspondents in foreign countries, have free access to foreign publications and programs." Chou barked the remainder: "You should not be naive. That spaceship is totally invulnerable to any weapon we know; it is immensely faster, completely maneuverable, altogether self-contained and self-supplying; by its photon drive, if nothing else, it can lay waste whatever areas the pilot chooses, with scalpel precision. Who controls those powers is master of the world. Do you imagine this has not occurred to the imperialist governments?"

"But, but the Sigman—"

Chou regarded Wang stonily for another while. And then, greatest surprise yet, he leaned back, smiled, took out a cigarette and struck it. Smoke streamed forth to accompany words gone mild:

"You have given insufficient thought to the ramifications, Comrade Professor. However, I daresay a pure researcher like you cannot really be blamed. Your work has been valuable. Now perhaps you can render a supreme service, so that men a thousand years from today will bow to your name."

Wang unclenched his fists. He felt abruptly weak. "I listen, Comrade General," he whispered.

"Chairman Sung and his advisers have analyzed the political implications of the Sigman's arrival. These are manifold. Before we can decide what to do, we need answers to any number of crucial questions. You, our most able and experienced investigator of the problem, are our present best hope for that."

Chou drew breath before he went on: "Some believe the Sigman will inevitably put itself at the disposal of the people's sacred cause, when communication has become good enough for it to realize what conditions are like on Earth. This is possible, of course, and pleasant to believe. But if theory stops at that point, the theorist reveals ignorance and laziness." Chou tautened again. Renewed cold fury lashed, this time beyond the office, around the world. "Can any educated person suppose the imperialists and revisionists have not considered the idea too? Have they no preparations against that contingency? Will they meekly surrender their profits and powers? You know better!"

"I, I do. How well I do," Wang stammered.

The image of his father limped across memory, wounded by the Americans as a youth in Korea, slain by the Russians as an army officer in Siberia. And the Soviet aircraft afterward, terrible snarling whistle when they slanted through the heaven of a little boy who wept for his father and screamed for terror. . . . *I nourished my hopes. I thought the slow opening of gates, the Tokyo Accord, the arms control agreements, the famine relief effort—such things seemed to me the harbingers of a better day, when China will no longer be ringed in by demons. And they may have been; they may have been; I do not doubt that the vast majority of people everywhere are honest and of good will.*

Yet Chou speaks rightly. Too sudden a dawn may alarm the demons of night to the point of madness.

Wang wet his lips. "We must proceed with utmost care, yes, I understand," he said.

"There are other possibilities," Chou told him. "Conceivably the Americans, for example, may find ways to lie to the Sigman, delude it into striking a mortal blow for them. Or, more likely, it will answer any technical questions put, never dreaming they are imperialists who ask. As Chairman Sung has declared, we cannot blindly assume that history on so different a planet followed an identical course with ours. For all we know, Sigmans have always been pure and peaceful Communists, or they may long since have transcended Communism itself."

"I will follow every word of every discussion in the

ship," Wang promised. "Should we demand a general moratorium on requests for engineering data?"

"That will be decided." Chou jabbed his cigarette forward like a bayonet. "It is even conceivable that the Sigman has evil intentions, or can be persuaded to evil actions. Wait! The laws of Marx, Lenin, and Mao must be applied imaginatively, not dogmatically. Suppose the Sigman's race did not build that vessel. Suppose the creature is a kind of pirate who stole the craft, after the trusting owners had provided instruction in its use. Have you never felt just a trifle suspicious of one who makes years-long voyages alone?"

"If it is alone."

"If not, why have its companions never revealed themselves?"

"Who can gauge the motives of a mind absolutely nonhuman?" Wang frowned. "I must admit, I have in fact often said, I am puzzled by its solitary traveling. Intelligence, sentience, by any reasonable definition we can make, must involve communication in the most fundamental way, might indeed well be said to *be* communication. For what is thought except the creation and manipulation of symbols? A primitive species with no instinctive drive toward communication—a drive actually stronger than sex, often stronger than self-preservation, as in a Communist who undergoes martyrdom to help spread the truth—a race without that kind of urge would, presumably, not evolve a human-level brain. It would remain merely animal. Therefore the Sigman ought to want companionship, conversation, moral support, like you or me. I doubt we could stay sane, Comrade General, if we had to endure so prolonged a loneliness."

"This is no time for lectures," Chou said. "You are directed for the nonce, first, to understand that your country may be in mortal danger; second, to lend your fullest efforts toward speedy guarding against any dangers—and, naturally, speedy realizing of the bright opportunities we hope will prove to be the reality of this situation."

Wang lifted his hand. "For the people!" The traditional pledge came forth briskly, but failed to stir his spirit. He wondered why, and decided that the stark response he had gotten to his jubilant tidings had downcast him.

"Push forward with your whole energy toward mastering the language," Chou said. "If we can stay abreast of the Americans in that respect—if, better, we can surpass them—they will not be able to hoodwink us or the Sigman."

"But the language is artificial," Wang objected, "and thus far is rudimentary."

"Then you must take a leading role in its further development."

"M-m-m . . . yes. As it grows, I suspect, in due modesty, I will become the most proficient in its actual use. Dr. Canter is brilliant, but her genius lies in theory; she lacks my practical experience with a variety of tongues. Serov, Duclos, and—"

"Indeed, indeed." Chou registered ardor. "At last you may become able to talk with the Sigman privately—if, for instance, no one else can follow the conversation—and explain the facts." He checked himself. "Let such decisions wait their proper time. The immediate requirement is to get full information. Can you phone Canter and ask her to send her material at once, no matter how chaotic it looks?"

"I can try," Wang said doubtfully. "Her superiors may already have forbidden it. Or, if not, she is . . . a very vulnerable person, I think, hiding in a brittle shell. She may not wish to show anyone else something of hers that is scrawled and disorderly." He paused. "Besides, might a call not seem overeager?"

Chou dragged on his cigarette. Reluctant, he agreed, "It might," and smashed the stub into a crowded ashtray.

"Frankly, Comrade General," Wang continued with more vigor—for reminded of the magnificent scientific romp ahead of him, he could forget about man's vicious lunacies—"I do not believe it matters. She gave me the essential information. My own notes are copious; and my office has received printouts of the latest recordings, as per agreement. Dr. Canter spoke freely to me, often unnecessarily fulsomely. We lack nothing except her precise mathematical analysis and the exact rules discovered by it.

"Do you not see, the insight itself is what counts? Now that we know what to look for, I feel sure we can duplicate her results in two or three weeks. Any competent analyst who has access to computers—"

"Excellent!" Chou actually beamed. "You are in charge. Work space will be cleared for you in this very building. Sleeping quarters will adjoin it. Commandeer anything and anyone you please."

"What?" Wang blinked. "I can operate from my home.

Or, if a large staff is required, my University department—"

"Comrade Wang," Chou said, happily more than severely, "I realize you are anxious to see your wife and children, but I fear the needs of the people come first. Security measures are essential; you know why. As you have probably guessed, this interview was ordered on the highest level of government.

"Your wife will be informed that you are detained on business." Chow paused. "If you, ah, find that biological urges distract you from your studies—"

"No, no," Wang said. There passed through him:

Not what he's thinking of, especially. In fact, let us be honest, here alone among ourselves, we several souls (for I do believe that many primitive tribes, and as subtle and powerful a folk as the ancient Egyptians, spoke a profound truth when they said that man has more than one soul)—my Yao, who was moonlight and mountain peaks, has become a dour fanatic whom I stay with largely because her impeccable respectability guarantees me permission to travel, correspond, read, listen, savor this entire marvelous world. (Until we have a system which grants the same freedom to all men, security tragically requires that only a few can enjoy it.)

Oh, I have further reasons. Men always do. I sense that down underneath the shrill voice and the tight lips, she too remembers; she too wonders, hurt and bewildered, what happened.

And do you recall, O souls, that conference in England (calligraphic austerity of Oxford's spires against iron-gray clouds a-race on an enormous wet wind), and the book with which I read myself to sleep one night, what was the author's name, yes, Chesterton, cranky, wrongheaded, already archaic a hundred years ago ... nevertheless he defined asceticism as the appetite for that which one does not like—? We have an element of asceticism in us, do we not, my souls?

He had been looking forward to his home simply as a place. He rated (the Americans would say) a house and garden well outside this city, built for a mandarin in Manchu days. The curve of branches across a full moon; the grand sweep of roof, paradoxical in the mellowness of old red tiles; shadows of breeze-blown flowers on a wall where hung a scroll of willows, bridge, mountain captured in a few swift lines eight hunrded years ago by Ma Yuan himself; the books, yes, old Li Po, the poet who was more drunk on life, really, than on the wine he sang of—

Before everything else Wang missed his children. P'ing. Tai and Chen were good boys, one took pride in Tai's excellent marks at school and his earnestness among the Pioneers, one felt sure Chen would outgrow the hobblede-hoy's loudness. But small, small P'ing (which sounds not unlike the word for crabapple that blooms red and white across the quickening earth, but which really means peace) came running and laughing to meet him, holding out her arms, squealing delight when he tossed her in the air; she walked hand in hand with him through the garden and called him a great big bag of love.

Well, a week, two or three maybe. No more. To help make sure that incandescent horror will never bloom above P'ing, that her melted eyeballs will never run down her cooked chubby face, that she will, rather, inherit the stars.

Wang grew aware that Chou was regarding him in puzzlement. A whole minute had gone by. He laughed, hearing it himself as shrill and uneven. "I beg your pardon, Comrade General. I was thinking and forgot— Yes, I will get busy at once."

"Good," Chou said. "We are fortunate to have you on our side. Tell me, do the Americans have anyone else to compare with this Canter?"

Surprised, Wang searched his mind. "Difficult to judge. They have extremely competent men. Levinsohn, Hillman, Wonsberg . . . Still, talents, capabilities vary. For example, Hillman has a weak heart; they cannot send him to space. I daresay, in view of what she has accomplished, Dr. Canter will remain their principal agent. Why do you ask?"

"However well-meaning herself," Chou said, "she reports to imperialists. We spoke of explaining the truth to the Sigman. Do you think the chance of doing this, uninterrupted, would be better in Canter's absence?"

"Why . . . perhaps . . . likewise hard to tell." Wang felt a twisting in him. She had talked so gladly. "It might be worthwhile trying to get her removed from the project. Suppose I— No, if I said, at this precise juncture, she was personally obnoxious to me, I would not be believed. . . . M-m-m . . . if we could prevail on someone else, a representative of some third country, to have a quarrel with her and— This is not my province, Comrade General."

"I realize that. I only wanted your opinion as to the desirability of easing her out."

The conversation went on awhile longer, until Chou

rang for a flunky to guide Wang to his new quarters. Alone, the general called an extremely important man and reported. Having received his orders, he next punched a button on the phone which activated a satellite relay to America. Scrambled after enciphering, the beam would if intercepted be taken for a burst of ordinary radio noise. That particular facility was as secret and rarely used as anything owned by the People's Republic.

The man who styled himself Sam Jones leaned across the table. "You know how a lot of us feel," he said. "We can't trust the Sigman monster. How can we dare? Next to it, the Chinks are like our brothers. Christ, it drips shit out of its whole body!"

"Yeh, I've kind of wondered myself," Nick Waller rumbled.

"And now this Canter woman. On the screen, in the papers, everywhere, you must have heard. She's found a way to talk to it."

"I heard."

The room was surrounded by night. Though the hour was late, a vibration went through, the huge noise of megalopolis. An overhead fluoro pocketed Jones' gaunt face with shadow. He shifted the briefcase on his lap.

"This has got to be stopped," he said. "You can see that. If we don't try to talk to the thing, maybe it'll give up on us. Whatever plans it has, it must need a way of talking first. Right? Otherwise it could simply flame our planet. It needs human dupes and tools."

Waller drew on his cigar and let the smoke out slowly, veiling his eyes. "Maybe," he said. "What you getting at?"

"I don't say the project will come to a halt without Mrs. Canter," Jones told him, "but it'd be handicapped, and we've got to start somewhere."

Waller stirred. "Who are you, anyway? All I know is, Luigi said I'd be interested to talk with you. How do you connect to him?"

"Never mind how," Jones said. "Don't be afraid of Luigi. Everybody has a hundred different connections. I could have traced you, gotten this appointment, through, oh, your mother if need be. She'd know a serving maid, who'd also work for a banker, who'd be a friend of a cousin of mine. You see?"

Waller grunted.

"What I'm after is professional help," Jones said. "I have a lot of information, but not much in the way of workers. The FBI— Never mind. I have a job for you which should be easy, if you want it, and the kind of money in this briefcase—more to come on completion of assignment—that I hope will make you want it."

Waller settled back to listen. He was not perturbed and scarcely curious. He'd need to make sure this Jones, whatever the real name might be, was not a police agent; but that wasn't hard. Nor should it be hard to cover tracks so well that, if Jones blatted afterward, the heavies wouldn't be able to prove anything about Nick Waller's company.

Okay, Jones was off orbit. What matter, if he had the jingle to pay for his whims? As many skewbrains as there were around these days, probably a few were bound to be rich.

Of course, Waller wouldn't commit before checking with his astrologer. But the horoscope would have to be pretty bad to deter him, who carried an amulet made especially for him by the local One.

"Go ahead," he invited. "Mind you, I doubt if I can help you myself. But maybe I can give you a name or two."

Standard operating procedure. The revolutionaries hadn't brought down the Ortho—it simply wore them out, in a generation of running guerrilla warfare—but they had brought a good many ideas, like new weapons and protective gimmicks and organization by cells, to the attention of the Underworld. Nick Waller had been a high school rebel himself.

VI

———◆———

Yvonne did not think she was timid: merely reserved, merely fond of her privacy and enjoying best those social occasions where a few good friends met for good food and conversation. She had expected to savor her triumph. And the congratulations, from personnel at Armstrong Base, by visiphone from Dad and Mother and the whole family, from the President and her colleagues around the globe, certainly they warmed her to the marrow. Yet they didn't quite make up for the stresses—the debriefings, the talks with assorted officials, the professional discussions, the cataract of requests for interviews, articles, lectures, support of worthy causes—finally the teleconference, when a dozen journalistic faces in their different screens threw a blizzard of questions at her weary head, many of them personal, and it was estimated that 100 million persons watched in the United States alone—

"Oh, please," she begged on the evening of her fifth day. "Let me go home."

Colonel Almeida nodded. "You shall, Yvonne. You look like death. I've been working to stall everybody else, clear your sked, so you can take a vacation. Get your duffel from your room and I'll flit you to Denver myself."

"My car's here."

"Leave it, unless you want to be mobbed by admirers, autograph hounds, newsmen, pitchmen, and whacks. Your conurb has practically been under siege, didn't you know? Better let me fly you. I'll have a man bring the car around tomorrow." Almeida drew a slip of paper from his tunic. "Here. Almost forgot. Your unlisted phone number. I took the liberty of arranging for it."

"You're sweet, Andy," she mumbled through the haze of exhaustion.

His Roman-nosed features broke into a grin. "No, just reasonably competent. I don't want you suffering the fate of the early astronauts and spending the rest of your career on the creamed-chicken circuit. We need you too badly."

He didn't press conversation on her in the helicopter. The ride was balm. Only a murmur of blades and wind, the gentlest quiver through seat and flesh, broke stillness. They flew high; stars surrounded the canopy, myriads aglitter in an almost space-clear dark, Deneb of the Swan, Vega of the Lyre, Pegasus, the Great Bear, and Draco, Draco curving its regal arc halfway around Polaris. The land beneath lay wide and mysterious. Now and again a constellation glittered upon it, some town where perhaps a few humans also looked upward and wondered.

When Denver's sky-glow had appeared, Yvonne felt sufficiently rested for talk. She reached after a cigarette, withdrew her hand—too much smoking, hour upon hectic hour; her mouth felt scorched and she might be wise to get an anticancer booster shot—and said, "Andy?"

"Yes?" His profile, vaguely seen against the Milky Way, did not turn.

"Why do you claim I'm needed? I'm not that important. Lots of people can carry on, equally well or better."

"Don't you want to?" His tone stayed level.

"Oh, yes, yes. But . . . all right, I made a breakthrough, but somebody else would have done the same eventually, and I doubt if the next big discovery will be mine."

"Think there'll be any? I mean, from here on in, isn't it a matter of developing language till we can inquire directly about things?"

Yvonne shook her head. The hair swirled over her shoulders and brushed her cheeks. "I suspect we're lacking another critical piece of the puzzle. Why hasn't the Sigman signaled us yet for a new delegation?"

"It never has, this soon after its last callers left."

"The situation ought to be different now. Given the expectation, finally, of real intercourse—" Yvonne heard Almeida chuckle, and felt herself flush—"well, wouldn't you or I carry on at maximum rate? No, I think the Sigman is waiting for something more. Until we have that to offer, it'll only spend odd moments on us, times when it isn't busy doing whatever else it came here for."

"You may be right," the colonel said. "You were earlier."

He paused, then went on gravely: "I didn't mean to raise the subject tonight, you being played out. But you seem a bit more chipper, and my superiors and I do want to start you thinking about it." Another pause. "Understand, nobody's mad at you. However, frankly, Yvonne, we wish to hell you hadn't reported your success on the way back, when the whole world could listen. And if that damned Chinaman hadn't been along— Given secrecy, though, we could have worked behind the scenes to influence his masters. You've no idea, I suppose, how wretchedly hard it is, reaching political or military agreements in a glare of publicity."

Surprise jerked her upright. "What? Andy, you're not serious!"

"I never was more serious. Look, Yvonne, you're a liberal intellectual, which means you're a reasonable and basically gentle person. So you assume everybody else is too. If only you'd apply to the rest of life the same rigorous thought and search for fact you do in your science!

"Consider. What the Sigman knows—or simply possession of its vessel—could give the overlordship of humanity to whoever got the exclusive franchise. Or if several factions acquired those powers, we'd be back in the missile era—worse off, probably, because I don't imagine we could cope with the problems raised by nonhuman technology, bursting on us overnight, as readily as for something we developed ourselves."

Yvonne decided to smoke after all. "Andy" she said, "I hadn't imagined you were stuck in ... in a cold-war attitude obsolete before you were born. Why, I've traveled from end to end of the Soviet Union myself and seen what they're like. Thousands visit China every year. And the arms-control treaties, the ... well, you must have read, seen on TV, been told, how the Soviets are undergoing the same kind of internal differentiation we are, the entire West and Japan are ... and the Chinese are beginning to. ... Andy, since before the Sigman came, for six or seven decades in fact, every major power has tried to avoid armed conflict. And when fighting did happen, no major power has tried for total victory. They haven't been that insane. And nowhere on Earth, these past ten years or more, has there been any conflict worth calling a war. Do you honestly mean that persons high in the United States government are still afraid of ... bogeymen?"

She sat back and inhaled deeply.

"Occasional bogeymen are real, my friend," Almeida answered. "Please listen. Please believe I intend no insult, I like and respect you, when I say you're stuck in an attitude which is worse than obsolete; it never had any relationship to reality. Sure, the Chinese are loosening up a bit, like the Soviets before them. In either case, the original religious fervor tended to die out with the original revolutionaries. Besides, experience showed that domestic terrorism isn't needed to further imperial ambitions, is actually counterproductive. Likewise, the nukes finally convinced the most foam-at-the-mouth fanatic that he couldn't possibly win in a rocket swap.

"None of this proves that the present leaders of our old rivals have renounced the old ambitions. Think of—oh, an example that doesn't look too partisan—England. The English had their Cromwellian period and outgrew it. Spreading the Gospel became simply one motive among many that sent their people forth. Nevertheless, they overran a large part of the world and wiped out a large number of non-English cultures."

"Today we have the Yellow Peril," Yvonne said sarcastically.

"Japan's also a Mongoloid country, and strong," Almeida responded. "Indonesia is getting there. I suppose we can leave the Africans out—though not for more than another generation is my guess—but sure, we face a White Peril too, not entirely Russian. West Europeans, Latin Americans . . . and, yes, Yankees. The Chinese, for instance, see us as posing a threat to them. They see themselves as the last wall between man and an insatiable American empire. Or have you never listened to a speech by Chairman Sung?"

"Rhetoric," Yvonne said in a fainter voice.

"Well—" Almeida drew breath. "Let me preach a bit, will you? Okay, you've been in the USSR, you've been to Europe and Mexico and wherever, no doubt you'll reach China eventually. May I point out, again with no putdown intended, you're not an intelligence agent, nor a sigaroon for that matter, you're a lady who travels first class? Of course you see only the pretty sights and meet only the charming people! I'm sure likewise that Wang Li admires you and has no fear of you. But does he trust President Braverman? Or General Nygard? Or lower-downs like me? I know damn well he does not. We've researched him. He's a Party member, probably not a fanatic but married to one; he's a captain in their military reserve; he's a Chinese patriot, steeped in Chinese culture, which was always xenophobic.

"Relax. My preaching won't include a sermon about

how I believe Western civilization and the American state are worth preserving, how they hold out the best long-range hope for mankind. Just grant me that a lot of men and women share my antiquated prejudice. And a lot of others share Wang's, and so on for every power bloc on Earth. The balance that keeps the peace is more fragile than I like to think about. The old fears and hatreds aren't dead. They're not even in a particularly deep sleep.

"The chance that *somebody* may get an instant ability to conquer the rest—don't you see how that forces *everybody* to grab for a monopoly if it can be gotten, for parity at a minimum—how the very scramble could touch off the arms race and the explosion? Besides a country, Yvonne, I've got a wife and kids. They won't go down the furnace if I can help it."

She stared before her. Denver's exurbs scrawled multicolored ideograms on a land now scarred and paved over. The central sky-glow mounted high, bright, and restless, like that cast by a city in flames.

"What do you want?" she said at last.

Almeida's words remained calm. "Well, if I had my druthers, America would acquire the monopoly. I think we can better be trusted than anyone else—maybe because I feel more at home among Americans. Failing that, we'll try to dicker out another arrangement we can live with. Doubtless at first we'll play by ear.

"The point is, Yvonne, from here on in, whoever we send aloft will have to work on our behalf, observe security, follow orders, give unconditional priority to the best interests of the United States." He hesitated. "They needn't be opposed to the best interests of humanity at large. From your viewpoint, Yvonne, better you on our team than some chauvinist. Right? From my viewpoint, I want the top talent available, and at the present stage, that's you. Think it over."

He became busy obtaining his route assignment from the aerial branch of Traffic Control. Yvonne sat silent. The lights of central Denver glared, blinked, crawled, swooped, leaped, drowned the last stars. Eisenhower Conurb loomed ahead, a mesa studded with torches. Almeida set down on the landing deck, sprang out, and helped her descend. At this level, the sounds from below were a muted rumble. A cold wind streaked by, ruffling hair and slacks, sheathing her face.

Almeida waved to the guards. Recognizing Yvonne, they didn't inspect her pass or check with whoever might have invited her. Almeida clasped her hand. Half shadowed, his smile was wry. "I didn't want to perturb you," he said. "Take your time recuperating. Call me if you need anything, day or night, office or home."

"I will," she said. "Thanks, Andy."

He climbed back into his machine. She walked toward the entrance. A guard approached, touching his cap. "Good evening, Dr. Canter," he said shyly. "Welcome back."

"Oh, hello, Sergeant Bascomb. How have you been?"

"Fine, ma'am, fine. Don't you worry. Seemed like a million people was trying to see you in your place, but we got them curbed and not a man among us that isn't bound to watch over your safety and privacy."

"You're very kind." Yvonne shivered in the breeze.

"Uh ... I wonder ... I got this kid, twelve years old, really wild about space. He thinks the world of you, after what you did. Would you maybe—?" The guard extended a notepad.

Yvonne smiled on the left side of her mouth. "Certainly."

The guard added a pen. "His name's Ernest. Ernest Bascomb."

When she was inside, Yvonne gusted a sigh. She felt, again, too tired for worrying over Almeida's statements, for anything except, *Now I can be alone!*

No need to leave the conurb; it was a complete community. No need, even, to be stared at in its restaurants, shops, theaters, churches, schools, recreation sections. Whatever she wanted physically could be ordered and sent by the delivery shaft, whatever her spirit wanted could be projected on a screen or duplicated on the ReaderFax or— *In two, three days I'll throw a party. A quiet little dinner, quiet talking, maybe*—she must chuckle—*maybe, in reward, a game of Scrabble.* Her friends had long refused to play with her, on the not unreasonable ground that they always lost.

An elevator, a slideway, another elevator, a corridor, her door. Under the system employed here, the chief of guards had its single magnetic key. Yvonne laid palm on scanner plate. The door verified that she was among those for whom it should open (in fact, she was alone in that class) and obeyed.

When it had slid shut again, she sent her clothes, including what she wore, down the cleaner chute, unpacked the rest of her suitcase, and stowed it. *Compulsive neatness,* she thought. *What I really wanted to do was drop the thing on the floor.*

She programmed the kitchen for a simple meal. Though she enjoyed cuisine and was herself an excellent cook, tonight she didn't feel like doing the job. Next she savored a hot shower. Emerging, clad in a woolly robe, she felt much happier. Her timing was precise, as usual; half an hour remained before dinner. Because of the state of her mucous membranes, she chose to relax with a martini instead of a joint, and because the water had made her deliciously lazy, she changed her mind about Beethoven's Ninth and dialed the hifi for Schubert's gentle, sparkling "Trout" quintet.

Leaned back in a lounger, among familiar furnishings, carpet, drapes, books, pictures, the last including an animation of Cape Cod surf that could never weary her, window framing a view of spectacular towers, music lilting, softness changing beneath her at every slight motion to fit every contour, she thought half drowsily: *Yes, life is good, on the whole. Those last two years with Cy, when we knew we were drifting apart and tried not to but couldn't do anything about it except quarrel . . . the final break . . . those hurt. Badly. However, they're behind us; neither would want to go back; I wonder if in time we may not become pretty close friends. . . . And Andy Almeida gave me a jolt. Let's be honest, his ideas may have a measure of truth. Yet not a full measure, surely, and nothing that can't be worked out. I do belong on the team. May I say "angels' advocate"? . . . Probably another man will come along, more understanding than Cy, and I hope by then I'll also have grown a little in understanding, in knowing how to give. . . . M-m-m, that noodle sauce smells great—*

The door chimed.

What? The guards weren't supposed to let anybody at her.

Well, they couldn't control her fellow tenants. Though conurb families characteristically held aloof from each other, she knew a fraction of her neighbors, had been to dinner and the like. If this was a celebrity-hunting stranger, she'd enjoy directing him to hell. Her lips tightened. But how could she escape the well-meant visit of a Sue Robbins or a John and Edith Lombardi?

The door kept chiming. *Could be urgent. If not, I'll claim a migraine.* Sighing, Yvonne hauled herself erect and walked to the scanner. She pushed the vision button.

While the face that appeared in the screen was unfamil-

iar, thick-boned and jowly, the body wore a blue Eisenhower uniform. "What do you wish?" Yvonne said. "I
asked not to be disturbed."

"I know, Dr. Canter," was the gruff reply. "I read the
orders board, and I'm sorry. Uh, this is kind of special,
maybe. Several of us in the guards, living and working
here in the same place as you, we decided we'd like to
show our appreciation. Nothing fancy, we know you're
tired and don't want company, it's just we can't send this
through the mails legal and a delivery tube seemed kind
of, well, cold." He held up a ribbon-wrapped carton of
joints. "This is your brand, isn't it, ma'am? Cuban Gold? I
won't stay a minute. Got to get home myself."

"Why—oh, how touching. You're too sweet." *I
wouldn't go through that much pot in a year. Still, why hurt
their feelings? That's an expensive blend.* Yvonne pushed
the admittance button. The door slid aside, the man
stepped through, the door closed again.

He tossed the carton aside and drew his left-hip pistol.
It was not the anesthetic needler, it was the .38 caliber
automatic, and the mouth gaped monstrous. She stumbled
back. A half-scream broke from her.

"Sorry, lady," the man said perfunctorily. "Want to say
your prayers?"

"No—no—go away—" Yvonne retreated, hardly able
to whisper the words, hands raised as if to fend off his
bullet. He followed. His coolness capped the horror.

"Nothing personal," he said. "Got a contract on you, is
all. Don't know from who. Maybe one of those warpheads
that go after anybody famous? Now look, I can't afford a
lot of time."

Yvonne stopped in the middle of the living room. He
did the same. Suddenly the spaciousness she had loved
became endlessness. A gray infinity of rug stretched about
her and him, toward walls gone unreal and receding like
distant galaxies. The breath sobbed in and out of her. The
music had grown tinny. Otherwise there was no noise, no
life, no help, nothing. Her garrisoned, soundproofed, auto-
mated fortress locked her off from the world.

She went through a moment's whirling and night. She
came out of it to find her intelligence clear and swift.
Terrar churned beneath—*this can't be happening to me,
to Me, Yvonne Philippa Berdt Canter whose family loves
her, who has talked with a being from the stars—
someday, yes, someday, more far off and hazy than those
walls—not this night, though, this night when the furniture*

is solid and my nose drinks plain cooking odors as well as the stench of my death-cold sweat—but she knew with machine calm that she had nothing to lose, and she heard herself ask:

"What can I give you to let me live?"

"Nothing," the man in blue answered. "I'd be dead myself too soon afterward."

"Ten minutes? Five?"

"I said you could pray if you want."

"I don't want. I want to live. My life's been too long in my head, I've denied my body too long." She let her robe drop on the floor and held out her arms. "Take as long as you want," she said.

"Huh?" The pistol jerked in his hand. "You crazy?"

"No. I'm buying two things, a little more life and something to fill it. The bedroom's this way." Yvonne turned and scampered across the rug. Her shoulders ached with the tension of expecting a bullet to smash between them. His footfalls came slowly behind. However bemused, he knew there was no rear door to the outside.

Yvonne ran into the kitchen. She unfolded the screen behind her and snatched a boiling saucepan off the stove. The jowly man shoved the screen aside. She cast the pan into his face and herself to the floor.

The gun crashed like doomsday. His scream was louder. He wabbled back out of sight, pawing at his eyes. "You bitch, you bitch—" She grabbed the dropped pistol and pursued him. He stood swaying. Noodles dripped grotesquely from his inflamed countenance. He got an eye open. "Bitch, bitch," he groaned and reached for his needler. She knew she was no markswoman. A heavy gun would buck and miss for her. She sprang to him, rammed the muzzle against his belly, leaned behind it, held it in both hands and squeezed. The explosion half deafened her. He lurched back. She followed, squeezing and squeezing, until after he lay fallen and jerked only because of the slugs' impact, until repeated clicks told her the chamber was empty and she could collapse shrieking into his blood.

VII

Almeida took a chair. Nurses passed to and fro beyond the open door of the otherwise private hospital room.

"A pity you killed him," he said.

"I'll have nightmares the rest of my life," she answered dully.

He patted her hand, which lay lax on the bed coverlet. "No, you won't," he said. "You're too sensible. You took a bad shock, and rest and tranquilizers are prescribed. However, I'll bet they discharge you inside a week. In fact, no one here cautioned me about avoiding excitement. That animal was overdue for killing. Don't waste sympathy on his hypothetical deprived childhood. Spend your goodwill on the billions who need and deserve it. Don't worry about legal complications, either. Your case has been closed. Not that it was ever really open. An Orthian defending herself against a murderer from the Underworld—the matter could've been a lot less clear-cut and the authorities would not have cared. They remember the revolutionary era."

"I've been told. But thanks." Yvonne stirred. "I don't feel too unhappy at the moment," she said. "Nor happy. My emotions are flat. Drugs, I know. In an intellectual way, I wonder what will come when I'm released and the drugs wear off."

"You'll see the incident in perspective and start enjoying life as before. Your therapist promised me on his reputation you would. He's handled really tough cases. Yours is practically routine, about on a par with a sensitive person who's witnessed a nasty accident."

"Well, maybe. I do plan to move. Not because I'm scared but because that apartment will always be where the thing happened."

"Sure, we approve. We'll help you find an address that can be kept confidential till this trouble's been disposed of.

61

That's why I said, pity you killed the swine. We could've gotten a lead. Might've had to narcoquiz, which would mean we couldn't prosecute afterward, but our real interest is naturally in who hired him and why."

"Have you any clues?" Yvonne asked with a flicker of interest.

"Well, an identification. Never mind the name. A known gunman, though he'd escaped conviction for murder; the time he served was for lesser offenses. The police are checking his associates. Military intelligence and the FBI are cooperating, plus following separate lines of investigation, which is why I keep saying 'we.' "

"On my account?" Yvonne shook her head. The gesture felt odd on a pillow. "The hirer must be simply a . . . madman. He probably believes the Sigman has designs on humanity."

"I hope that's true." Almeida's expression bleakened and his voice turned cold. "Bad enough if so. The Underworld's mercenaries don't come cheap. Your attacker was no chance-picked thug, he was a professional of gang war and criminal commando, almost a soldier. We've established that through our informants."

"Do you know how he got into the conurb?"

"Not for certain. He may have strolled into the public section, as if to buy something, and kept mingling with legitimate people in restaurants, stores, twenty-four-hour bars, that kind of place, till gossip told him you'd returned and he slipped on his fake uniform in a lavatory booth. If he acted cool, he'd've had a good chance of walking right by the elevator guard for the residential levels. But I suspect, instead, a front man rented an apartment in advance where he could den. We're checking on recent tenants, especially those who haven't been at home lately. Takes time, given the large and mobile population."

Almeida's scowl grew darker. "If a foreign power is out to do you in, Yvonne, hoping to delay our rapport with the Sigman, we're worse off," he continued. "They have agents in our ranks—well, seeing we have agents in theirs, I'd be surprised to learn different—and maybe they'll manage to keep track of what we're doing."

"Oh, Andy!" she said. "That's paranoid. How could I be worth a great country's attention?"

"You're being reasonable again," he chided. "The fact is, here and there various governments contain paranoiacs."

Yvonne was faintly surprised that she chuckled. "Who are out to get me."

Almeida sighed. "Let's not argue. Will you agree your safety is desirable?"

"I *won't* live under constant guard. You don't know how I've always pitied the White House family."

"I can guess." Almeida eased a bit and spoke around a slight smile. "Forcing you into a real nervous breakdown won't help us. And you could well be right, that this was a wild one-shot attempt. Would you consider taking a vacation in a safe spot for, m-m, two-three weeks or a month? Meanwhile we'll carry on our manhunt. If we don't succeed, we'll anyway have time to work out security measures that won't intrude on your private life."

After a few seconds she nodded. "Okay. My therapist does advise a trip. Mind you, no secret agent tagging along and staring at me. The mere possibility of there being one would drive me off the track."

"I was afraid you'd say that."

"Who knows, given peace and quiet, I might get a few fresh ideas. Have you a suggestion?"

"Yes," Almeida said promptly. "In fact, I've already arranged it, subject to your approval. I'll know you're safe, if you observe a few sensible precautions, and you'll know I can't have planted a bodyguard on you—not in such a close-knit, stiffnecked outfit. The *Long Sergent*."

"The what?"

"Flagship of a sea gypsy fleet, currently in mid-Pacific. She takes occasional passengers, in delightful accommodations, lots of fun—if and only if the admiral approves of them. In your case, he fell over himself to issue an invitation, soon's I called him. We can flit you there secretly."

Yvonne frowned. "Sea gypsies? I'm afraid I'd feel uncomfortable among Byworlders."

"The Vikings aren't, especially, in spite of their flamboyant name," Almeida assured her. "The most eccentric gaggle of ocean wanderers is nowhere near as far gone as the Amazons or the Creative Anachronists or—well, a lot of self-styled Orthians too, considering what odd little businesses they're apt to run. The sea has less tolerance for peculiar behavior than the land. Besides, it takes considerable capital to build a ship of the kind required, let alone a fleet. The Vikings keep no particular religion or social ideology or what-have-you. They're mostly a bunch of hardheaded Norwegians who decided that for them there was more freedom and elbow room and probably more income on the water than on the land. I'm sure you'll enjoy them. And you'll be safer than anyplace this side of Apollo Station."

Yvonne yielded. "For that long a speech, Andy, you deserve to win."

The big news broke the day after Skip had talked to Keough. "This changes every configuration," the Tuatha chief said. "Stick around awhile. I might wangle you a direct interview with Dr. Canter."

She had become the obvious target, especially after the general nature of her idea was described. It tied straight into Skip's hypothesis, convincing him he was right. Nevertheless, the owners of impeccable credentials were standing in kilometers-long lines—thought his metaphorically slanted mind—for a short visiphone conversation. What priority would a broke twenty-two-year-old drifter be assigned?

"Patience, son," Keough advised. "I'm making calls halfway 'round the world in both directions on your behalf. Not telling what your idea is. You've earned the right to spring that, and besides, you make it more convincing than I could. I only say you're worth listening to on the Sigman matter. You know, I never stopped to figure till you pointed it out, how many channels to how many offices I've got. My name's good among a hundred scientific and engineering leaders, and a percentage of 'em owe me favors. Chances don't look too bad. So, as I'd tell a Japanese about to commit hara-kiri, contain yourself."

Skip did, that first tremendous week, largely by wangling a temporary pick-and-shovel job which cast him into sleep each evening. The next several days, with nothing but rehash on the 'casts, were more difficult. When the announcement finally came that Yvonne Canter had sought seclusion after an assassination attempt on her, he tossed on his bunk the whole night. Next morning, red-eyed and tangle-haired, he bulled his way past underlings to Keough.

The chief was in the headquarters shack. The sophisticated gear of communication and computation stood incongruous against plain plastiboard walls and windows filled by a mountain. A breeze gusted through, bearing odors of pine, noises of machinery. Keough glanced from his desk. "Hullo," he said. "You're early. Sit."

Skip slumped into a chair. "You heard, sir?" he mumbled.

"Yeah. Right after the event. You know now they suppressed the information till they got things squared away. But my tentacles reach into the Denver police lab."

"And you didn't tell me?" Skip lacked the strength to feel indignant. "Well, this closes the direct route. Could you please start me on a new heading?"

"Contrariwise," Keough said, "you should consider it a lucky break, far's you're concerned."

"What?"

"I know where she is. I can put you there."

The word was like a thunderbolt. Skip could merely gape.

Keough looked stern. "I will, provided you make some promises. If you break them, you'll be kicked out so fast your guts will wrap around your tonsils; and I'll make a point of roasting you over a radioactive fire afterward. That woman's had a very foul experience, right on top of several days that must have drained her to the bottom. She is not to be pestered. Let her take the initiative. If you can't make her do that, come back here and we will begin over."

Skip swallowed. Tiredness dropped away beneath a quickening hearbeat. "Y-yes, sir. I promise."

Keough relaxed. "I figured you would. And I figure you can be trusted. I've been asking around about you, here and there. Okay. A good many years back, before I became boss of this tribe, we were working on the Great Barrier Reef of Australia. You may recall they had an international crash project to save it. Among the collaborators, for shipping and their special expertise, was a fleet of Norsky sea gypsies. I got friendly with a skipper who's since risen to admiral, and we've kept in touch. I mentioned your problem to him. The chances there looked faint. However, what the hell, why not invest a few minutes?

"My long shot paid off. He called me yesterday evening. Wasn't supposed to, but he'd given no oath, and when the American agents tried to browbeat him into accepting one of theirs aboard in disguise, he got his back up. That's an independent bunch of bastards. He knew I'd be discreet and that I wouldn't have sponsored you for no reason.

"That's where she is, Skip. In the middle of the Pacific Ocean, loafing toward Maury Station and Los Angeles, which last is where she gets off."

"And you'll flit me?" Skip breathed.

"Uh-huh. By the way, when he called me the admiral was undecided whether to admit you or not. I promised you'd tickle his crew's fancy. They don't see many amusing newcomers en route. That turned the balance, so don't let me down. What I'll actually do is give you a plane ticket to Hawaii and money to hire a private 'copter from there, plus modest expenses on board."

"I . . . don't know how to thank you, sir."

"Well, a cliché like that is not the way," Keough grinned. "Remember me when you're rich and famous. Seriously, I believe you're on to something important and the sooner you're given a hearing, the better."

Skip sat quiet a while. Finally he ventured, "I'd never have expected her to take refuge in the Byworld. From what the news accounts said, she's kind of, uh, spinsterish, in spite of having been married. Is that why they chose the fleet—for a hidey-hole nobody'd guess at?"

"Who says all the sea gypsies belong in the Byworld?"

"Why, isn't that what the word means? People who've left the conventional way of the Ortho but not gone into crime like the Underworld? I haven't made it to any argonaut community myself, but I've read and heard—like one of them belongs to the Mormon Revivalists, another to the Free Basques—"

Skip's recollection trailed on: *You have your ships built, nuclear-powered, loaded with the materials re-use equipment developed for bases on the moon and Mars, able to keep the sea indefinitely. You fish; harvest plankton; process water for minerals, weed for food and fabric; prospect the bottom for ore and oil, maybe under contract; do tramp cargo carrying; whatever's handy. Your brokers ashore haul away and sell what you've produced, buy and haul back what you need. You've registered your ships in a primitive country with bribable rulers; you take out nominal citizenship there yourself; the rulers pass laws which make your group, for practical purposes, a sovereign state that can do anything it wants, provided it stays within international waters and international law about stuff like navigation and conservation. . . . Hey, what marvelous luck! I get to see Yvonne Canter and a gypsy fleet!*

Keough's words reduced his excitement a fraction: "The Vikings are different. Sure, they fly the Pasalan flag, but just to get out from under the welfare state at home.

They consider themselves the respository of the old-fashioned Northern virtues."

"For which they stand four-squarehead," Skip chortled. He bounced to his feet. "Whoo-ee! I'm really on my way? Wow and yow!" He flung the door open and cartwheeled forth across the ground. He returned in a minute, playing "Sweet Betsy from Pike" on a harmonica snatched out of his pocket.

VIII

Massive, slow-spoken Admiral Granstad and family invited the passengers to dinner in their suite. Yvonne Canter was introduced as "Yolanda Cohen." Skip didn't contradict. Poor thing, she looked altogether empty, save for a ghost behind her eyes.

"Are you a student, Mr. Wayburn?" He could barely hear her routine-polite inquiry.

"No," he said. "I'm kind of looking around."

"Oh," she said. For the rest of the evening she spoke little, mostly when spoken to. He didn't see her in the next three days, except briefly and distantly. Though they were the only two outsiders, seclusion wasn't hard to manage. *Ormen den Lange* was enormous. Besides command posts and offices, it housed in ample quarters four thousand men, women, and children, schools, hospital, cultural and recreational facilities, and an astounding variety of small private enterprises.

Skip no longer minded biding his time. It brimmed with fun and fascination. His bachelor cabin, however comfortable and charmingly decorated, was simply to wash and sleep in. Otherwise he was exploring the ship and its half-dozen companions. The latter were more interesting technically; they did the work, whereas *Ormen* was like a floating conurb, linked to the rest of the planet in standard electronic ways. But the flagship had the sports and games, the delightful informal restaurants and taverns and live theater, the people.

These Vikings might exalt honest toil (well, actually, competent and conscientious use of the machines that did the toiling) and self-reliance. However, they weren't dour about it. Instead, they were as jolly a lot as Skip had ever encountered. The average upper-class Orthian was doubtless more hard-driving, well informed, thoroughly trained, including in the new mental disciplines which could evoke effective genius from ordinary cerebral endowment; but he was also anomic, chronically anxious, inwardly alone: a sane and realistic logician, emotionally crazy as a hoot owl.

The oldest Vikings kept youthful spirits. And the younger adults immediately swarmed over Skip. They spoke excellent English. He was the first sigaroon most of them had encountered. They reveled in what he could offer, and vied to interest and divert him in return. His first three nights after the Granstads' stiffish dinner, he was carousing till implausible hours. On the morning of the fourth day, a stunning blond nurse he'd met in the course of this invited him to eat at her place after she got off work. She made it clear that that wasn't all she was inviting him for.

Sure, let sunshine and sea air draw La Canter out of her shell. First she has to satisfy herself I can't possibly be a G-man. Dunno why she objects so violently to being guarded—touch-me-not personality reinforced to an unreasonable degree by her nervous condition, I suppose—but if it's a fact that the U.S. government had to accommodate to, I can do the same. Next she has to get acquainted with me. Well, okay. We don't reach port for quite a spell.

Intending to be properly rested for the evening ahead, Skip took his sketchbook and colored pencils onto a promenade deck. He was alone there; the population was at its jobs or in its schools. *My chance to try drawing waves, not making them.*

The scene cried for a thousand different pictures. Below the bleached mahogany and ropework safety rails of this high place, the superstructure fell down, fore and aft, occasionally rearing back aloft, in a many-shadowed intricacy not unlike a pastel-and-white, streamlined Grand Canyon. Often its severity was relieved by miniature parks or hanging gardens. Beyond, the remaining fleet was strewn across kilometers. The lean-hulled service vessel paced closet; a hum from one of its machine shops drifted to him. Farther out, a squat factory ship processed kelp harvested elsewhere; water roiled white at the intake and exhaust pipes of a mineral-extractor craft; the trawler was more distant, almost on the gigantic circumference of vision. The sea surges were wrinkled, foam-laced, royal blue shading to clear green under the crests and soft almost-black in the troughs, forever moving, alive with change, like the blood in a man's heart. Diamond dust gleamed and danced, cast by the sun out of a gentle sky where two or three bright clouds drifted.

Stabilized, *Ormen* was free from roll, and its nuclear engine made neither smoke nor noise. A low vibration did pervade the hull, again reminding Skip of the pulse inside himself. The ocean rushed, boomed, hissed, laughed, beneath a lulling cool wind that carried odors of salt, iodine, ozone. The wind rumpled Skip's hair and tried to play with his sketchbook. He swore at it cheerfully because he liked the song it blew, of the leagues upon leagues it had fared and the wanderings still to come.

"Good morning, Mr. Wayburn."

He turned, caught off guard by the soprano voice. "Uh, good morning, Dr. Can—Miss Cohen." *Damn! I was supposed to play along unless/until she admits who she is.*

She regarded him fairly calmly. "Canter, were you about to say? You're not the first. I do resemble her. Not surprising. We're second cousins."

"Oh. Well, I will be unique and not bug you for details about your famous relative," answered Skip, giving thanks to any gods who might expect it. "I'll bet you've scarcely met her."

"You'd win your bet."

That she could lie thus easily indicated she was making a fast recovery. Furthermore, while her tunic and slacks formed a prim contrast to the sloppiness of his coverall, their buttercup color must reflect a degree of cheerfulness. Her lost weight had just begun coming back; high cheekbones and arched nose stood forth hatchetlike. Yet the ponytailed hair shone ebony, the tilted and really rather lovely eyes were no longer dark-rimmed, the lips—their remaining paleness not hidden by cosmetics—curved in a smile that was small, a wee bit frightened, nevertheless a genuine smile.

"I didn't want to avoid you," Skip said, "nor bother you either. The admiral's wife told me you need a rest."

"I hate to ... seem rude," she said hesitantly. "Mrs. Granstad told you aright. Finding you when I came up here—" She groped out a cigarette from her beltpurse and struck it.

"Please don't think you have to make conversation. In fact, I can leave. I've plenty else to keep me out of mischief, or in it as the case may be."

Her smile revived, a little larger. "Yes, I noticed you off and on. Cutting quite a social swath, no? And I see you're an artist."

"Gnawing away at it. I'm afraid these billows of mine won't give Hokusai much competition."

"May I see?" she asked. He handed her the book. She studied his sketch with what he believed was appreciation. "Why, that's excellent. The way you catch the interference patterns— Have you more? May I look through?"

"If you want. Mainly they're doodles. Or cartoons. I drew this, for instance, on the chopper that brought me here."

A laugh, weak but a laugh, broke from her. The picture showed two real Vikings, in horned helmets and ringmail, who stood on a fjord shore watching a longship sail past. One said to the other: "He's a pretty peaceable fellow, you know." The figurehead on the ship and the tail on the sternpost were those of a mouse.

"You could sell such things, I'm sure," she said.

Skip shrugged. "Sometimes I do, like to a small-town paper. The big periodicals take too long to reply. Chances are I'd be elsewhere when they did, leaving no forwarding address."

"Indeed?" She returned his book and inhaled slowly of her cigarette, studying him edgewise. "How come?"

"I'm a sigaroon. Migratory jack-of-miscellaneous-trades, entertainer, you name it and I'll tell you what to feed it."

"Pardon me, you look too young for that."

"Younger'n I am. I turned officially adult four years back. That's when I went on the wing."

He had tried it almost two years earlier, but had been caught. The officer who made the arrest took him for a ratpack type and administered a skillful beating. Because his restlessness had brought ever more friction into familial relationships, his parents consented to his three months' commitment to a juvenile rehabilitation center. There the authorities weren't cruel, but he was soon ready to vomit with boredom.

Why mention it? What embitterment had been in him was long since blown out by the many winds he had felt.

"And you're obviously well educated," Yvonne Canter said.

"A lot of us are." Skip explained the background and philosophy of his part of the Byworld. She was a good listener. "I've lots of respectable friends," he finished, "including the man who arranged for me to visit here."

He could guess her thought: *An influential friend, to arrange his passage simultaneously with mine. Not that the Vikings are bound to obey directives from the Ameri-*

*can government. They find its goodwill useful, though. . . .
Well, he seems pleasant and harmless. I won't complain.*

Skip's task was to make himself more than "pleasant
and harmless" in her eyes. An awkwardness had descended. She said lamely, "I wonder where their submarine is
today."

"They collect manganese nodules off the bottom," he
replied. "I was told it's scouting for new territory, like the
farmer's cat."

"What?"

"Nothing," he said in haste. She might find the joke a
trifle too earthy. "You know, Miss Cohen, I'd be glad to
do your portrait if you'd sit. At your convenience, naturally, and you could keep the result. You have an exotic look
that challenges me."

"Oh? How?" Pinkness crept into the ivory cheeks, and
the lashes fluttered. She was not so far off the human
female norm that she didn't enjoy a compliment.

"Hold still a minute, please, and I'll try to show you."
He flipped to a fresh page. Clutching book and pencil box
in the left hand, he circled back and forth around her,
crouched, cocked his head, finally settled on an angle of
view and started drawing. Though she had finished her
smoke, and perhaps wished for another, she held her pose,
stiffly and self-consciously.

His pencil flew, leaving a trail of curves and shadings.
He had intended to glamorize as much as he guessed he
could without insulting her intelligence. But as the picture
grew, the concept did likewise. *Erase this line, that shadow, damnation, they're wrong! She* is *beautiful—austere
beauty, half abstract, like Death Valley or a Monterey
cypress bent and strained by a century of storms.* "Excuse
me, I've had a misfire, would you hang on for an extra
two-three minutes?" *Better not make those comparisons
aloud. She'd doubtless misunderstand.* "There! Thanks a
googolplex. It's rough, but maybe you can see what I
saw."

He ripped off the sheet and gave it to her. She made a
low noise of astonishment. Color mounted and sank in her
face. Her index finger searched along his perspectives. He
had done more than subtly emphasize her best features, he
had captured a quality of bowstring tautness. The slightly
Oriental cast of countenance remained, but the clothes
flowed back around bosom and leg in a manner to recall
Nike of Samothrace, and the rail behind her was shown

from a point which made it clear that she was looking into the sky.

"I never ... Remarkable," she breathed. "You make me appear more strenuous than I am—"

Oh, no, Yvonne.

"—or am I reading something in that nobody else would? What a souvenir!" Her glance dropped. "If it's for me," she said uncertainly.

"Why, sure, if you want," Skip told her. " 'S nothing more than a cartoon, in the original sense of the word." Outrageous, the idea bounced through his mind of adding the Sigman and a caption. ("Now what did it mean by *that?*" Or. "Does its language consist *entirely* of smut?" Or—) "I'm really trying to sell you on letting me paint you," he reminded her. *Your portrait, I should say, though you know, when you've put on a few more kilos I could have fun— Whoa, horsie.*

"I'll have to think about it. Your offer is most kind, of course." She struck a fresh cigarette. Hastily, as if to steer conversation from herself: "You must have earned by your talent occasionally, Mr. Wayburn. Besides casual sales of drawings, that is."

"Call me Skip, will you? Everybody else does. Complicates matters here, it meaning 'ship' in Norwegian though pronounced about the same as the English word. . . . Yeah, I have gotten commissions here and there. I've grown a tad cautious about accepting them, after some trouble one landed me in, a couple years back."

"What happened?"

"Longish story."

"I've nothing to hurry for."

Good! That means she's enjoying this chatter of mine. Keep it up, boy.

"Well, you see," he began, "I chanced through a tiny Southern town, not Byworld exactly, but more fundamentalist than is easy to believe in this day and age. In fact, everything there was half a century or worse out of date. They even had a jukebox in the diner—ever seen one? The Sigman, by being rude enough to exist, had upset the faithful like a tornado. They had a reaction going that would've put a Colossus rocket in Lunar orbit. I fell talking with the owner of that diner. He meant to close for a week and call on his relatives elsewhere. I suggested he let me brighten his bleak little p'ace while he was away. We settled on a price for a Bible scene.

"I didn't let anybody in before the grand unveiling, and

I cooked and slept there when the fever had really grabbed me. I did patronize my friendly neighborhood moonshiner. First time I came back from him, I looked at what I'd begun, and realized what a noble opportunity I was missing. All that space, and I planned to do the Sermon on the Mount? Ridiculous! Not that Jesus lacks possibilities, but I haven't clarified them for myself and see no sense in copying someone else's ideas.

"When I woke next morning the zeal was still in me, proving that however drunk she was last night and hung over today, my Muse was authentic. I laid in a supply of jugs and for the rest of that week, half out of my head from lack of proper food and sleep, plus superabundance of corn squeezin's, I painted the best thing I'd ever done, maybe the best I'll ever do, the Revelation of St. John the Divine.

"Angels in the four corners, ceiling high, emptied vials of wrath upon the jukebox, the television set, and the doors to the ladies' and gents' rooms. God the Father burned with glory on that ceiling; his long white hair and beard tossed in the storm of destruction, like his robes, and his face was half human, half lion. The Son on his right hand was less successful—I wanted to show that he pitied the damned he was helping cast into eternal fire— well, he came out more like a grimly satisfied revivalist saying, 'I told you so.' The flames around the thrones— not hellflames, mind you; modeled on solar prominences— reached up around the Holy Ghost, whose wings carried their leap farther. Gabriel I modeled on a film I'd once seen, a trumpeter 'way back in the jazz era, Bix Beiderbecke; he was obviously blowing riffs, syncopating, having the time of his immortal life. The rest of the angels, the elders, the whole divine crew, were distracted by his concert. Some were annoyed, trying to concentrate on their work, but a couple were listening in totally goofed-out ecstasy. Me, I had the time of *my* life with the zoo around the throne. . . . I'm babbling."

"No, no, do continue," she said, her gaze never leaving him.

"M-m, well, etymology aside, why should murals not include floors, considering how tough the modern paints are? This floor became Earth. The dead were rising out of it. You saw tombstones falling, graves opening, the whole scene chaotic, since I guessed that by Judgment Day every spot on the planet will've been used a thousand times for burials. I doubted the resurrection of the flesh would be instantaneous so I showed different stages—a recent corpse still half rotten, a skull rolling to rejoin its verte-brae, two skeletons squabbling over a shinbone, ancient dust starting to whirl into the first ghostly outlines. . . . And the completed cases! I didn't try for tragic dignity, like the Orpheus Fountain in Stockholm. Revelations is a wild book, utter lunacy. The weaker among the resurrect-ed were painfully trying to haul themselves upright with the help of the counter stools. A couple of lovers were crying for joy in each other's arms, yes, but they were old when they died. Remembering that in heaven there is no marriage, a young couple was trying to sneak a quick—ah —well, a cowboy and an Indian were kicking and gouging, and you can imagine the rest.

"Along the lower part of the front wall I put a distant view of burning cities, floods, earthquakes, and similar calamities, including a lightning bolt that struck a funda-mentalist church. On the right wall, the saved were whirl-ing upward like dry leaves in a cyclonic wind. Most I modeled on happy drunks, happy potheads, et cetera, but some looked dubious, some bewildered, one was thorough-ly airsick. Naturally, everyone was naked. Scripture says nothing about restoring shrouds. On the left wall, the damned were similarly tumbling downward. Hellflames were roaring aloft to greet them, and the first few had begun to sizzle, oh, that was not nice. Nor were the devils who hurried them along. I'll spare you details. Satan himself was better-looking, in an ophidian way. One hand reached out to rake the sinners in, the other made a fist at God, middle finger extended.

"Behind the counter, for the delectation of the trade, was a further view of the opposition, the Great Whore of Babylon on her beast. I wrote the number of the beast in binary. She was glad-eyeing the Antichrist, and I made it perfectly obvious what he had in mind. . . . No, sorry, I don't want to offend you."

Skip's apology was *pro forma*. She was giggling. "Oh, my, oh, my," she said. "How did the town react?"

"A-wing and awash as I was, it never occurred to me they mightn't appreciate my masterpiece." Skip sighed. "I had to justify my nickname for sure, that day." *Not the first or last time I was glad to be good at karate and kendo.* "No doubt the owner repainted."

She sobered. He realized that the verve of his account had been due to more than gusto, and that she noticed this. "Odd," she said slowly. "I never met anybody before who had art in the blood."

"Takes the strangest forms," he tried to quip. His reference escaped her.

"Competent illustrators, of course," she went on. Her gaze moved from him to the water and back. "Two or three who bragged about their dedication and were not competent. None were real artists, the way I've known several bone-real musicians and scientists. Until you today."

Dare I take the opening? Yes—carefully, carefully. Jet back the microsecond she registers distaste for the subject. "I thank you," he drawled. "Me, however, I suspect no person alive, no human who ever lived short of maybe a Rembrandt or a Bach, compares in ... artistness? ... to Earth's distinguished guest."

Did she flinch? He couldn't quite tell. But raised brows questioned him.

"The Sigman." Skip pointed skyward at random.

"Well, m-m, Canter—" she couldn't help blushing—"Canter does, you know, appear to have proved the being insists an esthetic standard be met. Like, say, a Heian period Japanese nobleman."

"Not what I'm getting at, though Dr. Canter's work does suggest my notion may not be too skewed."

"What is your idea?" Now she was merely being courteous, he assumed; yet she didn't sound resigned.

He was reminded of how you played a game fish on a thin line. "Aw, nothing much." He turned, leaned on the rail, stared out across the waves. "A sigaroon-type idea."

She moved to stand beside him. "Go on, Skip. Do."

He struggled to sound calm. "Maybe I'm dead wrong," he said. "I think I know what the Sigman came for, what it's doing, why it's hardly paid attention to us, how we can make it sit up and wag the tail it hasn't got and declare that nothing is too good for the human race. Extravagant of me, no?"

He risked a sidelong glance. The profile that intrigued him was turned seaward, the ponytail fluttering back in a strengthened breeze. He hadn't scared her off. She did grip the rail tightly, and her voice was a trifle strained: "Tell me."

IX

———◆———

She dropped her incognito for him the same day. They maintained it in the presence of others, except the Gran stads, whom they seldom encountered. This cost Skip the friendship of the blond nurse, who started wondering why he spent hours on end with that skinny Cohen woman, old enough to be his aunt—well, *years* older than him—that he could have spent with her. She didn't take kindly to his explanation that Miss Cohen had a wonderful mind.

Oh, well, there'd been a few almighty enjoyable nights. And he kept on playing an occasional game of ball or bending an occasional elbow with the rest of the younger set. Though equally puzzled by the change in his behavior, they didn't ask him the reason. Individualism would not combine with close quarters and need for disciplined co-operation unless you added the catalyst of respect for privacy. Doubtless they decided that one must expect eccentricities in a sigaroon.

Skip quickly got on first-name terms with Yvonne. They were both afire, exploring the consequences of his hypothesis, laying plans, making preparations. Barring the unforeseeable, she was pledged to stay in the fleet to Los Angeles. Colonel Almeida and company needed that long at a minimum to arrange for her safety. She fretted, until she discovered how she and Skip could put the interval to use. *Ormen* could draw on data lines, computer banks, worldwide visiphone service, as readily as her workroom at home. The ReaderFax could print out a copy of any item in any important library anywhere, with any degree of fidelity for which the customer was ready to be charged. There was even a Mitsui Sculptor, to do a similar job for three-dimensional objects whose scans were on file. Normally these were statues and ceramics, but Skip insisted on it for paintings, and hang the expense.

"Texture's more important than people realize," he

said. "They don't know how sensitive their own vision is, trained or not. The fact's most obvious in oil painters who put on thick daubs, like many Impressionists. Don't think it doesn't matter for others, though. They can be as slick as Dali, but that surface is not optically flat. Same for Oriental inks and water colors. In them, the cloth or paper becomes part of the composition." He hesitated. "Uh, Uncle Sam will reimburse you for those we've ordered here aboard for examination. Won't he?"

"Silly," she laughed. "I can debit him directly."

They stood on the fantail, late after a day of projecting image after image on the screen, making choices, continuing to debate these while they went out for dinner. Nobody else was here astern. The throb of full speed was tranquil in the ship. Above shone stars, and a moon that built a bridge over darkly sheening waters and turned the wake into a white river. The lights of a companion vessel glowed tiny and jewel-colored across kilometers. The air was mild, quiet save for that low beat of engines, the rush and gurgle of passage. Yvonne and Skip leaned on the taffrail, side by side, gazing aft and drinking peace.

"Good," he said. Musingly: "You know, I've wondered if modern repro is altogether a desirable development. I mean, look, if you can have a Leonardo or Monet or whatever in your living room at reasonable cost—not a print from a photograph, not a copy by some hack, but in essence the real thing, every shade and contour identical—well, won't you? Instead of traveling thousands of kilometers to break down your arches in a gallery?"

"Y-yes. At home I collect Matisse and Picasso . . . and Byzantines, by the way."

"What I wondered about is, what's going to happen now that the modern artist has to compete this directly with the masters of two or three thousand years? I see us these days as on the brink of a renaissance. You know what absolute garbage-pit bottom we hit in about the middle twentieth century, don't you? Or have you been spared? I see a new idiom with all sorts of potentials, a blend of Western, Oriental, aboriginal, and scientific motifs, I see it beginning to develop. Will it get the chance, though? Will enough aficionados pay for it? And the artist himself, surrounded by overwhelming greatness—what'll that do to him? One reason I went on the wing was to try and get back to life itself and find how *I* look at things."

Yvonne patted his hand. She smiled in the moonlight.

"You're an idealist." At once, as if frightened, she withdrew the touch and reached into her beltpurse.

"Who, me?" His ears grew warm. "Lady, no! I do what I want, not a lick more if I can help it. You're the service-to-mankind specialist in this duo."

She took forth a pack of joints and offered it to him. "Thanks," he said. "Reckon we could both stand a relaxer, high-keyed the way we are." They struck and inhaled. "Although," he continued after the first tingly breath, "you thrive on work. You were like a spook when I met you. Now, a week later, on the job ten-twelve hours a day, you've fleshed out, you don't jump at shadows, you joke—"

That was not entirely true, he thought. She appreciated humor of certain kinds, but hadn't much of her own. And, while physically she was about back to normal—which he enjoyed seeing—her nerves could still attack her. As now. The red end of her cigarette trembled between her fingers, waxing and waning with inadvisably quick, deep drags.

"Did I say something wrong?" he asked.

She shook her head. Pain edged her voice. "Not your fault. You accidentally reminded me. I am not altruistic. If only I were, just to the average extent, I wouldn't have made the total mess I did."

"Are you kidding? Yvonne, you've done tremendously."

"Have I?" The pot must be grabbing hard and fast, in her exhausted state, for her to let down the barriers so. "I killed a man. I see his dead face before me, pop-eyed and slack-jawed in bewilderment. He'd be alive if I'd simply wounded him."

"Huh? I knew a boltless nut tried to murder you, but the newscasts never—"

She told him, in short harsh words between inhalations. At the end, tears rivered down her cheekbones, turning them silver in the moonlight.

He clasped both her shoulders and said: "Yvonne, listen. You're not to blame. Not an atom's worth. You were scared out of your wits. And you'd no experience with guns, had you? That must've been a double-action weapon. You can empty the magazine in seconds. You didn't have *time* to know what you were doing. And you did nothing evil anyhow. You were defending yourself. The world needs you. The world is better off without that creature, that thing."

"That human being, Skip."

"Come off it. Shooting's an occupational hazard in the

Underworld. Would you feel sorry if the incident had happened to a stranger and you heard about it?"

"This happened to me! Y-y-you've never killed a man. Have you?"

"No. I've come close. And I always carry a fang. Illegal as typhoid, but I sew a hiding place into every pair of pants I buy, and I keep in practice. If someday there's no choice, sure, I'll open him up. Which'll cause me neither pleasure nor remorse."

"You're telling me the same as everybody else." She turned and looked back out to sea. Skip let his right arm slide down around her waist. She sighed and leaned lightly against him.

"Sorry." Her tone was muted, rather slurred. "I shouldn' wish my troubles on you."

"I'm honored to help, if only as a convenient shoulder," he said. "And I don't pass on what's told me in confidence."

"Thank you, Skip." She smiled, however forlornly. Her eyes remained fixed straight before her. "I'm healing 'bout as fast's the therapist predicted. I don' often think 'bout ... that ... any more, an' it's rarer yet I feel guilty. Soon I'll stop al . . . al-to-gether. Doubtless, awhile af'erward, I'll stop wondering if I do wrong not to feel guilty." She let out a slow, smoke-scented breath. "This b'longs to a whole complex of troubles I've had throughout life. Be glad you're 'n extrovert. Introversion's no fun. My marriage disintegrated b'cause I saw too seldom that he needed more of me 'n I was giving. An' do I really want to be as alone as I am?" She tossed the stub overboard. "Hell with it. I'm stoned. Better go to bed."

He escorted her to her cabin. At the door, in the empty, ventilator-murmurous, drive-quivering corridor, she smiled at him, unsteady mouth and imperfectly focused eyes. "You're a darling," she whispered.

He rejected temptation, bowed and kissed her hand, and left with a single "Goodnight."

They had taken to meeting on the promenade deck each forenoon, to walk around it for an hour and discuss their work. Skip reported there next day, unsure whether Yvonne would. She did, though later than usual, stiffly striding. "Hi," he greeted. "How are you?"

"Fine, thank you." He could barely hear her, and her look avoided his.

" 'Fraid you might've been sick," he continued glibly. "Contrary to folklore, people do get sick from an overdose of mary jane, and we tied one on last night, didn't we? At least, I did. Can't remember too well—hazy recollection we said things which seemed important but probably weren't—drugs are sneaky when you're not a regular user."

She gave him a quick, startled glance. "Do ... do you feel ill, then?"

"Not bad. The judge gave me probation." They started their walk at a brisk pace. The wind blew loud and chill, the waves ran heavy and gray-green, under many clouds. *Ormen* had entered the Japan Current.

"Let's lay the art question aside for a while," Yvonne proposed, more quickly than was needful. "I've noticed you don't seem to understand how Sigman biology differs from terrestrial. The facts may suggest something to you."

What is suggested to me, he thought, *is that you want a safe topic—art being concerned with emotion—till you get over having bared yourself. Okay.* "Well, I know the chemistry's another. Where analogs exist, amino acids and whatnot, they're apt to be ... mirror images of ours ... isomers, is that the word?"

Yvonne took a cigarette: tobacco, of course. "I'm thinking about cellular organization," she said. "The biological specimens we were given were both plant and animal. A few of the plant samples were of more than microscopic size, none of the animal. But the animalcules included both protozoans and metazoans—single-celled and multi-celled—and there were several grams of tissue that may be from a member of the dominant species. Naturally, our scientists failed to culture or cultivate anything, and the cells didn't look similar to any of Earth. Some cytologists claim they've identified what corresponds to chromosomes, ribosomes, et cetera. Others dispute this. No matter for now. The broad general principles seem roughly the same. Don't they?"

"I reckon," Skip said.

"They aren't! The metazoans are put together completely unlike the main terrestrial kinds."

Yvonne paused. A whale broached a ways off. Skip thought: *The human beast has redeemed itself to the extent of establishing halfway decent conservation policies. How shoddy my life would be with no miracles like that yonder!* "—easiest explained by starting with—" *Oops, I forgot.* He made himself pay heed to the woman.

Her lecture might be a shield for her; nevertheless, she delivered it well:

"—the conjectural development of such organisms on Earth. I'm not a biologist, I may get details wrong, but here is how I understand the idea.

"The original aggregates of cells must have been mere clumps; something like them survives in algal ciliate balls. They went on to become hollow spheres, often two concentric spheres, like the modern volvox. But presently—this was still in the Pre-Cambrian era, remember—such spheres developed specialized inner and outer walls. They had an opening at either end, for intake of nourishment and excretion of what they could not use. From simple gastrula like that is descended almost every kind of animal we know. Some formed mere colonies, like the sponges and corals. But others joined end to end, becoming the first segmented worms.

"From those early worms in turn"—Skip refrained from the obvious double pun—"evolved all the higher forms. In an elaborated version, we keep to this day that old, basic tubular-modular structure. The bilateral symmetry, the oral-digestive-anal tract, the ribs and vertebrae show it. Even branched-off organs like heart and lungs adopt the canal principle, though the lungs have become sacs—well, I needn't illustrate further.

"This isn't the only way to evolve biological complexity, I'm sure you know. Plants haven't followed it. And if we've been given a fair sample, no Sigman life has. Perhaps the closest terrestrial analog to it is our ductless glands.

"Here on Earth, certain protozoa swim by means of cilia, hairlike processes along their sides. Something similar exists in what we have seen from the Sigman planet. But not identical. Those protozoans typically are not flat but spheroidal. The cilia are spaced over the entire surface, and they are for more than locomotion. They whip the water, and any organic matter it may contain, toward the cell. The animalcule has no particular intake or outlet; its skin is permeable, and the currents raised by the cilia force the foodstuff through to the interior. Oh, more is involved than that. Chemical action on the membrane probably breaks down the larger molecules to smaller ones that can pass in, and interior processes must be extraordinarily complicated. But our biologists would need a great many living specimens to trace the details."

Yvonne stopped for breath. Skip said, "I can guess

what's coming. Yes, I remember vaguely reading an arti-
cle. My private life at the time was overloaded with new
impressions and— Point is, when these Sigman mircrobes
decided to join forces, they held hands instead of kissing."

He was pleased to see a flash of grin. "You would think
in those terms," she said. "Yes, they linked some of their
cilia. These lost the original sweeping function and became
tubes for support and for the conveyance of fluids. In
various parts of the tissues our people have studied, the
tubes have shrunk till the cells are in direct contact. But
this is for special purposes, as we use independently swim-
ming blood corpuscles. The basic Sigman metazoan structure is a lattice of spheroids held together and integrated
by rods. The rods may be solid, hollow, or permeable;
they may be rigid or flexible; that depends on what their
particular function is. The topology remains the same. So
does the permeability of the cellular skin, however
modified this has been here and there in the course of
millions of years."

They walked a lap in thoughtful silence. A Viking
passed by. *"God morgen, du,"* Skip hailed. His accent
wasn't bad. The sailor responded. Skip returned to his
brown study.

"I believe I see where this leads," he said at length.
"Check me out. The basic symmetry is not bilateral, it's
axial or radial. There's no tendency, anyhow much less
tendency than here, to develop a definite front and rear
end. You get much less development of specialized organs,
too. The permeable cell can take in its own air and water
vapor—it's kept free cilia, developed into efficient little
fans, am I right?—and, uh, it excretes waste products
directly and continuously. Our Sigman friend needs claws
to break down solid food, but only to the point where the
juices seeping from the surface between those claws can
reduce it to a mush that dissolves and passes on up the
arm. They must be even fiercer than our stomach acids,
those!"

"You catch on fast," Yvonne nodded. "It's thought the
same juices probably circulate throughout, in diluted
form—the main protection against disease germs. As for
physical protection, the skinless lattice would be hopelessly
vulnerable, except that probably most land animals have
staggered pinecone shingles like our space traveler. With
air and water passing freely between, the animal isn't
insulated from sense impressions, the way a lobster or

turtle is. Therefore the evolution of intelligence isn't inhibited."

"Uh-huh," Skip said. "And with four stalked eyes in addition, and who knows what other extensible organs, I'll bet the Sigman experiences more than we do. Our only cells that make direct contact with the environment are in the breathing apparatus, parts of the food tract, and the skin, and those last are dead on top." Excitedly: "The Sigman's whole body does! I'll lay odds that if you limited it to human capabilities, it'd go bonkers. Sensory impoverishment."

"Oh, there must be many qualifications and exceptions," Yvonne said. "For instance, it must have a brain."

"Must it?" he challenged. "As we understand a brain? Why can't those not very specializing cells carry nerve impulses too? Maybe the Sigman thinks as well as senses with its entire body. If that's true, I envy it. . . . M-m, a less compact layout than our cerebral whatchacallum. Signals take longer to cross. The Sigman 'ud think slower'n us. Which might not matter on its planet. Animals that want to make a lunch off it have the same handicap. And gravity's weaker. You have more time to recover from a stumble or dodge a falling rock."

Yvonne halted. "Why—you may be right!" she exclaimed. "Among the features I found in the language was that it does have considerably lower rate of information transmission."

"I recall," Skip answered. "Given the enormous sensory input, however—if we aren't building theories in midair— well, I'd guess it thinks more deeply than us. We're quick-witted but shallow, it's ponderous but profound." He beat a fist on a railpost. "Hey, hey, hey! How *about* that? What type of artistic conventions would develop— Zonk! Wowsers!"

He capered whooping around the deck. Finally he stopped before her and burbled, "You were inspired to raise this subject. We've got to explore the notion further. C'mon, let's inspire ourselves with a morning beer in Olav's pub. A single schooner apiece. Two at most. All right, you win, three. If the sun isn't over the yardarm, we'll have them lower the yardarm for us." He tugged her arm. She resisted. "Come *on*, robin!" She did.

Maury Station rested on the continental shelf off the Oregon coast, about fifty kilometers out and as many fathoms down. The Vikings had a cargo of refined metals to deliver. *Ormen*, too huge for the docks, anchored at a safe distance amidst its followers, except for the concentrator ship. That one laid along the assigned pier, which projected from the caisson-mounted platforms supporting a complex of buildings and machinery.

Unloading would be quick, but Granstad had promised a six-hour stay for the sake of children who had never toured the place. The rest must keep out; their numbers would swamp the available facilities. Most of them had visited Maury or similar colonies before. And the fleshpots of Los Angeles, where organic products were to be landed, were now only a couple of days away.

A few men wangled leave to go off hydrofoiling, scuba diving, or dolphin riding under the aegis of local youths who frolicked about the vessel on their big fish-herder animals. Yvonne regarded the splashing, leaping, and shouting wistfully. "I'd enjoy that," she said.

"Water's cold hereabouts," Skip warned. "The merfolk are used to it, we aren't. True, you get warm fairly quickly in a wet suit. . . . Well, why don't you? We're passengers, not under orders, nothing to prevent. And any boatman or diving guide or dolphin boy would come snorting like a grampus to oblige you." Their relationship had reached the point where his habit of speaking little gallantries to any good-looking woman didn't embarrass her. This was the first time in a week or more that he had seen her slightly unhappy.

She sighed. "I mustn't. Andy Almeida would be furious. He insisted I stay aboard, incognito, the whole trip. For safety's sake. I couldn't be Yolanda Cohen here. Not that I've ever been to Maury, but it's crammed with scientists and some are statistically certain to have met me at Triple-A-S conventions or wherever. My earlier work had applications to cetacean pseudo-speech." She squeezed his hand. "I talk too much. You go. Have fun."

"Do you yourself think you're in danger?" he asked.

"No," she said emphatically. "If the attempt on me wasn't a case of mistaken identity or something, then it has to have been the work of a lunatic-fringe anti-Sigman group. Those are known, and I'm sure the government has put the fear of the Lord in them."

"So does this Almeida own you? Will a squad of police meet you at the gangplank?"

"He wanted that, but I wouldn't have it. He gave in when I pointed out that, precisely because no one will know where I've been, no assassin can be lurking."

"Right. Well, take my word, you're a blessed sight safer in Maury, with the sea laying nine or ten atmospheres of pressure on you, and killer whales which are supposed to be tame flippering around loose, than in Los Angeles. I've not been here either, but I know LA and I've read about Maury. They're your breed of cat, come from all over the world to study and conquer the seabed together. How can they threaten you?"

"I'd ... I'd hate for the news to run ahead of me. A crowd of journalists would be almost as bad as a melodramatic killer."

"Okay, we go first to the director and arrange precautions. Confound it, woman, I want to see the place and I suddenly realize you can get me entree to parts I'd never be let into by myself. Let's fare! Right away! No, don't stop to change your vests. You're dressed for energetic sightseeing and I doubt they ever notice who's wearing what in an R & D station."

She let herself be swept along. They descended the ladder on *Ormen*'s clifflike side. Skip whistled and waved at a passing boat. The pilot was glad to give them a lift in exchange for a bit of gossip. From the upper structure, they took an elevator down the shaft to the central undersea dome. Five minutes afterward, they were in the director's sanctum. Three of the minutes had been spent in finding it.

Burly and shaggy amidst a clutter of oceanic memorabilia that filled walls and overflowed floor—books, pictures, instruments, an old-time diving helmet, corals, mounted fish, harpoons, God knew what—Randall Hightower pumped Yvonne's hand till Skip wondered if water would gush from her mouth, and boomed welcome. "Sure, sure, m'lady, nothing's too good for you. I'll record a notice, for hourly replay on the entire intercom system: You must avoid strain and you don't want publicity and will they please not get on the phone to Uncle Oscar in Keokuk or Cousin Ching-Chang in Shanghai for the next few days, to blat that they personally eyeballed Yvonne Canter. They'll understand. You can trust 'em. You know what inhibited closemouthed rabbits we scientists are. I still think of myself as a scientist. Somebody's got to administer this chaos. I sneak off to my lab when I can. Experimenting with production of alcohol from plankton. Bigger things are under way in Maury, of course. Alison!" He gave his pretty secretary, who was standing by, a pat on the bottom. "Man the guns a while. If anybody insists his business with me can't wait, drop him in the Mindanao Deep. I'm going to show these people around."

"The announcement," Yvonne reminded him.

"At once, Dr. Canter," he said worshipfully.

The remaining hours were sheer marvel. The central hemisphere was surrounded by a ring of others. These were connected by tunnels and kept at ambient pressure, allowing swimmers to pass in and out through simple airlocks with no need for compression or decompression. To go between them and the middle dome naturally required time in a chamber. Besides atmospheric density, composition must be altered, at a rate which allowed the body to adjust. The helium content made voices shrill to the point of unintelligibility. It was an experience to hear Hightower roar squeakily. He supplied his guests with headsets that stepped down sonic frequencies. The merfolk didn't bother. They were used to the upper range, and were gradually evolving a set of dialects adapted to it.

In two-three hundred years or less, Skip thought, *a whole new undersea civilization.*

Windows in the compression chamber looked out upon dimly greenish-lit waters, here and there brightened by lamps or flashbeams; on crusted rocks, upward-waving green-and-brown kelp, fish, crab, lobster, shellfish, squid, fishlike humans passing, bubbles astream from the McPherson "gills" that extracted oxygen for them, a sounding orca and a man directing it— *A whole new world,* Skip exulted. *Arts like none that landsmen could imagine. When I settle down at last, why not a seabed colony? The biggest already have room for wives and kids. Surely a painter could be squeezed in somewhere— and Charlie Russell didn't have a wider-open range to fence with canvas!*

When laboratory workers engaged Yvonne in conversation, he found pleasure in the shapes of the scientific apparatus. He found ecstasy when Hightower gave him and Yvonne a ride in a superglass submarine. When finally they must return and the Vikings sailed off, he chattered to Yvonne over dinner as if he had been blowing pot or downing gurgle, except that she thought his talk really did verge on brilliance. His gaiety infected her. Afterward they went dancing in the Bellman Club, with champagne on the side.

At her door she said, holding hands, "Thanks for a wonderful day. Your initiative made it."

"Thank *you,*" he replied. "Mainly for your company,

but for the magnum too." He had no more resented her buying than he would have resented buying for her if he'd been flush and she broke. "Not to mention everything else I've enjoyed because of you. What an all-time faring this has been! I'm sorry it's about to end."

"We'll be going on, remember," she breathed.

Her eyes, her lips, her slight sway forward, could not be misunderstood. The kiss lasted longer than most, and she was better than he had expected.

They broke apart. She opened the door. He made a tentative move to follow her. "Goodnight, Skip," she said gently. He stopped. She lingered a second. He couldn't tell if she wished he would insist; she was the first top-grade Orthian he'd had anything meaningful to do with, and eight years his senior to boot. "Goodnight," she repeated. The door closed behind her.

Oh, well, he thought. *Maybe later. It'd be—I dunno— another dimension for something great—or am I simply curious?* Unaccustomed to brooding over his own emotions, he let the speculation die and sauntered to his cabin.

"No luck, eh?" Andrew Almeida asked.

"None," responded the face in his deskphone screen. "Every combination of man-Sigman phrases, beamed on every reasonable frequency band, starting with the one on which it signaled us when it originally arrived . . . all drew blank. Not a flicker in return."

"Ump. Can radio pass through those force screens, do you think?"

"If the Sigman can transmit, which it did three years ago, it can receive. No, I suppose either it hasn't recognized our message as a plea to continue building communications, or its interest in us remains barely marginal, or it has a motive we can't comprehend."

"Damn!" Almeida gnawed his mustache, which reminded him it was approaching an unmilitary length. "Well, at least the Russians and Chinese and the rest have failed too."

"Do you think they tried?"

"I know they did. We maintain reconnaissance. Besides, didn't we try?"

The scientist bridled. "Why are the nations duplicating their efforts? For that matter, Colonel, why have I been instructed to report to you alone?"

"The first question answers the second," Almeida told him. "If I have to repeat the briefing you got when we instituted security here, you should consider submitting your resignation."

Wang Li looked up. His wife was home early from her solidarity meeting. Moonlight came in the doorway around her, striking shimmers off the mother-of-pearl insets that ornamented his old, dragon-carved ebony chair. A breath of dewy jasmine followed, and chirring of crickets. She snapped the door shut and switched on the fluorescents. He blinked.

"Why were you sitting in the dark?" she demanded.

"Good evening, my dear," he said. "How was the assembly?"

"If you had been patriotic enough to attend, you would know," she answered.

He averted his gaze from her tall, gaunt, drab-clad form. "I am still tired after the language assignment. We had no mercy on ourselves."

"You never attend if you can avoid it."

"Not my function. 'From each according to his ability.' Besides, tonight I have a difficult matter to think through."

Yao was silent half a minute. Then, mildly, seeking to be reconciled with him, she said, "Oh, I see. Can you tell me what?"

He shifted about in his seat. "I must compose a letter to Yvonne Canter. She cannot be reached by visiphone, but no doubt a letter to her at Armstrong Base will be passed on when she comes back from wherever she has fled."

"Surely you need not ask an American's help." Yao walked closer, till she stood above him, and touched his cheek.

"I might. Remember who had that first insight. In this case, however, I wish to express my regret at her bad experience, and assure her that we, her Chinese colleagues, are overjoyed that her esteemed person escaped harm. But it is not an easy thing after all, because—"

Her indignation returned on wings. "What! An imperialist—" She broke off. "I understand we must maintain the courtesies," she said. "Why is a formal note hard to write?"

"It should not be formal. She may well think that that cowardly attack on her was instigated by our government."

"Let her, if she has a persecution mania."

Wang's fingers strained together. "And she could perhaps be right," he said around a thickness, while he stared at the floor. "My every attempt to ask was met with bland denials, until I was called before General Chou and informed that further asking would be considered evidence of deviant thoughts. Yes, I realize disproof may be impossible. I cannot be shown details of our intelligence operations. Still, I am not a wholly unimportant man. Why could no one take the time to explain to me precisely why disproof is impossible in this particular case?"

He raised his eyes and saw shock livid on Yao's countenance. "You dare say that?" she gasped. A screech followed: "You dare call our leaders murderers?"

His temper broke. He sprang to his feet. "Be quiet!" he shouted. "I will not be named traitor, I who serve beyond the sky! What do you do for the people? You nag and pettily tyrannize a few score wretches who might instead be busy at something useful! Leave me! I do not want to see you again this night!"

She covered her face and ran. He wondered if she would weep.

Poor Yao. Grief welled in him. He sat down like an old man. *If she had let me explain before my worn-out nerves gave way ... I can imagine—I do not believe, yet I can imagine—that a decision was made to kill Yvonne Canter, not in hatred, not in callousness, but because the imperialists would use her to gain their ends. If I truly thought that, I would kill her myself, with these hands.* He saw them open and empty on his lap. *I do not fear her. I fear those whose ancestors in spirit forced opium on mine, sacked Peking, bombed Hiroshima, slaughtered and slaughtered to block the liberation of Korea, Malaya, Vietnam, Thailand—the list goes on too long—who blocked liberation by a wall of corpses. And I fear the Soviets who killed my father and bombed my land; I fear the Europeans and Japanese, fat, bustling, smug, who could so quickly turn back into hungry demons; I fear whoever might burn my P'ing alive, and it is so easy, so gruesomely easy to make a nuclear weapon ... and now that spaceship, like a vulture wheeling over this fair, living Earth. ... Poor Yao. Poor Yvonne Canter. Poor mankind.*

X

Reapers of the sea, the Vikings could not have kept a schedule had they wanted to. Not until the last short leg of her voyage did Yvonne know the precise date on which it would end. She arranged for the duplicated paintings to be posted to Armstrong. The government would justifiably have balked at meeting the bill for having them copied over, especially after Skip turned in his list of what else he wanted, pictures he had never been in doubt about and other items like figurines, Asian bowls, and a Grecian urn. "I may as well give you my luggage too," she told the purser.

"Hoy, keep a suitcase," Skip said. "We aren't hopping the first jet for Denver."

"I'm not sure about that," she answered against her will. "I've been thinking and—"

"Aw, come on. Don't back out of your last chance to be a free woman. I know places here that the tourists never see, and I don't refer to respectable back yards." He tugged her sleeve. "Do. Throw a toothbrush and a change of vests into a bag, same as I've done, and hang onto it. Hurry, if you want to watch us dock."

She surrendered. "I'm a bad girl. The colonel will be horrified. And he's a nice man, really."

"What you need," Skip grinned, "is practice in badness. I'll train you. Let's lift off."

The scene topside was impressive. The blue glister of San Pedro Bay was nearly hidden under swarms of ships, tugs, barges, fisher boats, yachts, police and watercleaner craft. Private and commercial helicopters filled heaven; beyond them, contrails crisscrossed white and thunder drifted down. Ahead stretched the immensity of the megalopolis, a thousand pastel hues of buildings checkered in green by parks, pierced by spirelike skyscrapers, knit together by soaring arcs of railway, each detail diamond-sharp through Los Angeles' crystalline air until vision was stopped by the curvature of the planet. The sound of men and machines flowed outward, a deep steady querning that reminded of the tides or of the bloodbeat in some enormous animal.

It was hot, and sailors were abustle. Skip and Yvonne found shaded refuge on a lower deck. "What are these untouristy places you speak of?" she asked.

" 'Fraid we won't visit the most interesting," he said. "They're too bloody interesting, and I don't mean British bloody." At her inquiring look: "I once knocked around in local Underworld circles. I wasn't joining them, I was simply the bouncer in a tough nightclub. That led me to know several full-fledged Underworlders, and after I helped one in a fairly nasty fight, he took a fancy to me and— Forget it. I don't want to make noises like a romantic hero. Truth is, what I saw and heard was what decided me to move on, in spite of liking it where I worked."

Since he was happily observing the action, she could let her gaze dwell on him—disposable tunic purchased aboard, the extreme flare in the collar and red in the color proclaiming its cheapness, worn with as much dash as if it and the faded trousers and scuffed shoes were the latest mode from Rio; cowlicked brown hair, freckle-dusted brown face, boyish nose, mobile mouth, eyes big and green and the alivest into which she had ever looked. Why had he, child of long roads and the weather, liked spending his nights in smoke and din and the breath of vicious morons? A girl, beyond doubt. Or girls? She could imagine that body, hard, supple, and warm, giving joy to a whole chorus line.

She could imagine herself in that chorus.

I'm not falling in love with him, am I? The thought was dismaying. Or was it? She asked hurriedly, "Where do you propose we go?"

"How 'bout Afroville for lunch and browsing? Sure, you must've been there, but I'll bet you ate only at nationally advertised restaurants and talked only with shopkeepers."

"No," she said, "mainly I was at its university, conferring. They have the best sociology department in the country, which includes a couple of first-chop linguists. My colleagues were, are somewhat bitter about the ethnic façade. They don't want their community known as a variation on Chinatown."

"Then those prominent sociologists ought to get off

their prominent duffs and discover how much more there
is to a Chinatown than tourist traps. As for Afroville, I
guarantee your lunch won't be standard prettied-up chit-
lin's and collard greens, and it'll be cheaper to boot."

She bit her lip. *How can I say what I must?* "You . . .
had better watch your expenses . . . till we have you on
the government payroll," she forced out. "Unless you'll
. . . let me be debited. A loan, if you wish, till—" She
ground to a halt, her cheeks burning with more than the
light splintered off the water.

Skip gave her a surprised glance. "What's wrong?" His
puzzlement cleared. "Oh, yes. Male pride. Sure, Yvonne,
you keep track and bill me after my first pay crediting."

How will he survive in the Ortho? she mourned. *It's not
for the light of heart and feet.*

*He won't, and he doesn't care. When he grows tired of
running in the squirrel cage, he'll hop out, accept no more
reward of cashew nuts imported, roasted, and salted; he'll
merrily go back to his woods where acorns grow for the
taking.*

*I am too conditioned to the cage and the cashews. Nor
can I forget that the cage is connected to a shaft which
keeps the world turning. If the world stopped, the forest
would die.*

The ship was warped against its pier. "Get ready to
dash," Skip said. He took their suitcases. They had already
spoken their farewells and could debark with no more fuss
than showing proof of citizenship—credit cards would
do—to the machine at the gate.

She dreaded seeing a man from Armstrong or being
accosted by a polite official agent. But it didn't happen,
perhaps because of the deft way Skip maneuvered them
through a warehouse rather than the passenger reception
area. When they were on a muni train and it had rolled
from the station, she let out a breath and a shaky laugh.
"Now I am irredeemably a bad girl," she said.

"We'll make you worse," Skip promised. He consulted a
displayed map. "Change at Lomita and we can catch the
Harbor Express straight through to Afroville. Uh-huh."
Turning to her: "You haven't made clear how long a time
you can spend."

"I haven't been clear about it myself," she said in
confusion. "I suppose . . . if we take an evening flight to
Denver—"

"This evening? You josh."

"I—really—"

"Well, we'll see how the bones fall." Skip leaned back.
He obviously plans to tempt me. Do I plan to be tempted?

If we stay over a night or two or three ... separate rooms? If we stay, he'll take for granted that we—we— He won't be angry if I say no. Not him. He could pretend not to remember what I said that night on the fantail, and is still pretending to believe that I believe him. He might be hurt—no, I can explain how the trouble is in me, not him. I can do that much for him.

After I've gone to bed, he may stroll out and find somebody else. But he won't insult me by introducing her next day. Unless— He might not realize it was an insult.

"For a person on an escapade, you're tol'able glum," Skip said. "Smile." He twisted about on the seat, put thumbs at the corners of her mouth, and lifted.

She gasped. He dropped his hands. "I'm sorry," he said.

"No. Nothing. You surprised me." She took the nearest of those hands in her own. Sunlight, smiting through the window, turned the hairs on his knuckles to gold. How tough the palm was! Her words fumbled: "I've been a prickly pear these past few years, but it wasn't intentional, it just happened." *Is that true?*

"A condition to remedy." His free hand cradled her chin. He smiled into her eyes. She wondered in near panic if he would kiss her in this carful of people. He let go after a moment. She did too. "Lomita ahead," he reminded her, and rose.

Their change-train took a cigarette and a half to arrive. Meanwhile Skip suggested she stick her card in a cash vendor. "They use cash a lot in Afroville," he said. "Why not give me a thousand? Easy sum to recall I owe you, and I can play grand seigneur the rest of the week on that."

"Dare you carry so big an amount on you?" she asked.

He shrugged. What he lost, he'd earn back eventually, he assumed. She gave in. A kilobuck wouldn't damage her account. She drew more than a hundred a year after taxes, and had no one to spend them on but herself.

They boarded the express. It accelerated to a smooth and noiseless two-hundred kph. The cityscape reeled hypnotically past. Yvonne lost other sensory awarenesses, staring out.

Why not? My whole body wants to. Oh, it cries to!

The world would goggle and snigger to learn that Yvonne Canter was living with a twenty-two-year-old boy.

The world needn't learn. Almeida would make certain her address stayed confidential; probably she'd reside under her alias. He himself wouldn't care, might indulgently smile. The rest who'd know—to hell with them. The very cold hell she had a talent for consigning people to that she disliked.

But did Skip have more in mind than a few days' romp before they reported for duty? He liked her, he admired her intellect, he wanted to paint her portrait—

"Do you feel warm, Yvonne? Want to move over onto the shady side? You look like you're blushing."

From temples to breasts. "No, I'm comfortable."

—in the nude?

Why not a romp, then? What harm could it do? Afterward they could decide. . . . But if the decision was to end the relationship then and there, how much would that hurt, for how long? . . . And if they did go on a while, at last he would grow restless and kiss her and depart whistling some or other tune he'd have been whistling while he painted her, and would that leave her hobbling around the rest of her life on chemical crutches, and if so, would it have been worth it?

Or can't I too be casual? Must I forever work, even at joy?

Or could I make him want to stay, if that turned out to be my dearest wish?

The train glided to a halt. "Watts Towers," Skip said. "Here we are."

They checked their luggage and stepped forth into dazzling light. Behind them, the people's park mushroomed with the amiable eccentricities of its high structures. There must have been twenty, no two alike. A group of youngsters was gleefully at work on yet another.

Before them, palms lined the main street. It was reserved for pedestrians and the wagons of many children; the "sidewalks" were for bicycles. The buildings, all one- or two-story, were each surrounded by a garden. Colors blazed from the walls and the often conical roofs. The functions were wildly mingled—homes, a number of which had their own businesses in a front room, among shops, offices, small manufactories, restaurants, bars, theaters, a church, a mosque, and more and more. Folk sauntered, laughed and chatted, sat on their porches and plucked guitars, bought roasted ears of corn from a pushcart, stood in their storefronts and chanted the wonders of what they had to sell. Dashikis, tarbooshes, and lap-

laps were less frequent than the *National Geographic* inti-
mated; however, a brand-new style was common, a
flowing gauzy cape embroidered like butterfly wings, that
Yvonne guessed the entire Western world would soon be
copying.

The flower-scented warmth seemed to bake unhappiness
out of her. She clapped her hands. "Enchanting!"

"The cliché Afroville," Skip said. "Run by some of the
shrewdest people on two feet. Mind you, I don't put this
part down. You can find unique stuff here, handicrafts
especially, likelier to be honest value than what comes in
through your home delivery tube. We may as well wander
till lunchtime."

Yvonne had worried about being recognized, but Skip's
reassurance was sound. "Nah. The sensation's died of old
age. Your picture hasn't been on a screen for two or three
weeks. Ninety-nine percent of the population has lousy
memory, which is why circumstantial evidence is generally
better and fairer than eyewitness testimony. Unless somebody's looking for you specifically, or we chance on somebody who knows you personally, no one will pay attention. You stayed pseudonymous on the *Long Serpent,*
didn't you?"

She enjoyed herself in the shops and couldn't resist a
snakeskin belt. And the Black History Museum had added
a nautical section since she was there last; the Vikings
ought to see those juxtaposed models of the bronze-age
canoe from Denmark and the medieval ocean-goer from
Ghana. Lunch became late.

That was in an offside section, mainly residential. They
were the only whites. The restaurant was tiny, on a
trellised patio riotous with bougainvillea, rustling with
bamboo, splashing with a fountain that sprang from the
uplifted trunk of a stone elephant. A young man sat
crosslegged and produced unbelievable flams and paradid-
dles on his bongo drums. "No entertainment," Skip said.
"He feels like it."

The handsome waitress did not surprise Yvonne. You
always got live service in Afroville. But then Skip rose
and cried, "Why, hello, Clarice! Remember me?"

"Hey, Skip, baby!" They hugged. Nevertheless Yvonne
got the impression that, while neither would have had any
objections, they had never been lovers. *Maybe I think this
because I've read that Afroville has a higher proportion of
couples who are formally married, and the marriages*

*average a longer life, than in the Ortho of any Western
nation. Or maybe I want to think this.*

"I figured you were in Australia yet, Clarice."

"I was. You've been away longer'n you've counted.
Want to swap brags?"

"Sure do." Skip performed introductions, wincing the
least bit at "Yolanda Cohen." Yvonne remembered him
remarking, "Sigaroons don't lie among themselves as a
rule. If I'd rather not tell a friend something, I say so and
he accepts." While the food was being prepared, and after
Clarice had brought it, she sat down, drank coffee, and
conversed.

Yvonne almost regretted being too interested to pay
due attention to the meal, which was superb, especially the
ham-stuffed Brussels sprouts. *Furthermore,* she thought,
I'm too wistful. Clarice was not a female equivalent of
Skip; her roots in Afroville struck firm and deep. But she
had traveled, and not by careful first-class conveyance—
shank's mare, bicycle, motorbike, car, truck, bus, train,
chopper when she could wangle it, horse, camel, and once
a zebra—from Yukon to Yucatán, Copenhagen to Cape-
town. Her Australian tour had been in a semi-amateur
theatrical group, playing the outback more than the cities.
Between jaunts she worked here and studied chemical
engineering at the university. "Meant to land a job in a
desalination plant," she laughed. "Turns out they prefer
employees who don't take my kind of leaves of absence.
No harm. We're gettin' more of our own industry all the
time. Or maybe I'll teach."

In her absence, Skip said meditatively, "There goes the
shape of the future, or I miss my guess. We're not headed
into an age of speed and steel. That's already behind us.
We'll use its capabilities otherwise. The old Egyptians
learned tricks that're still handy to know, but we don't
build pyramids any more, do we?"

Yvonne thought of Almeida's fears, and thrust the
thought from her, stood up and said, "She makes me hope
you're right. Excuse me a few lambshakes. Which way is
the ladies'?"

A vendor in the room offered Just Before mints, twen-
ty-five for a new dollar. Yvonne demurred. Then: *Why
not? They won't commit me, he needn't know I have
them, they'll merely give me the option.* Her coin rattled
down the slot. She stuffed the roll into her beltpurse and
washed her face to cool it.

Clarice suggested the newcomers end their afternoon in a nearby amusement park. They did. Yvonne was slightly upset by a holographic animation in a plastidome labeled "Grandpa's World"—less by the phantom hippies, protesters, peace marchers, rioters, embattled policemen and college deans, lecturing professors, roaring orators, and the rest of that section, than by the giggles and guffaws of the mostly teen-age visitors. *Youth is cruel. Even Skip?* However, the astronautical division was tasteful; her spirits could not but rise with the great rockets. Back in the open, they found the usual shows and rides and, miracle, an old-time carousel or excellent facsimile, complete with sentimental painted scenes, calliope music, and animal figures to be whirled on.

They had supper in a Mexican restaurant. "Tell you what," Skip said over the last wine, "let's unhock our bags and skite down San Clemente way, junction up in a little beach hotel, start the morning with a swim and maybe go to Catalina."

"All right," she said, more huskily than intended. "That sounds like fun."

They walked out hand in hand. She knew that if he hailed a taxi and they snogged on the way to Watts Towers, she would share his bed. But that didn't occur to him. His merriment on the shuttlecar suggested to her that she might anyhow.

At summer sunset, the Towers station was moderately crowded. Skip wrinkled his nose. "Too much racket and bustle for me," he said. "Well, the LA-San Diego line is pretty good. We can be in our room, window open to the surf, in an hour." He started toward the storage area, not noticing her expression. She followed automatically, her world gyrating. *What did he mean? Anything? Everything? What should I say?*

Skip opened their locker and took the suitcases out. A man who had been seated on a bench approached them. Quietly dressed, he was an unobtrusive man unless you took heed of his lithe gait and hard features. "Dr. Canter?" he said. "How do you do? Excuse me, please. I'm Gerald Lasswell of the United States Secret Service." He showed her an identification card and returned it to his folder.

She stood wondering numbly why she felt so very numb.

"What's this about?" Skip demanded, annoyed.

"Are you with Dr. Canter, sir?" Lasswell asked. Skip nodded. Lasswell quirked lips in a tight brief smile. "We had two men to meet you in port," he said at Yvonne, "but somehow they missed you. Admiral Granstad told us you'd spoken of touring in this area. Our best chance seemed to be to post a man at every station. We have searchers out too." Roughly: "It's that important. Thank God you're safe."

"Suppose you tell us what the matter is," Skip snapped.

Lasswell shook his head. "Not in a public place, sir. Would you both come along to the office? The chief will explain."

Yvonne looked at Skip. "Should I?" she heard her voice ask.

"I can't force you, short of noncriminal arrest," Lasswell said. "Wouldn't you agree, though, Dr. Canter, neither my service nor Colonel Almeida is given to hysterics? You were nearly murdered. Now we have more information. I've sat here since morning and sweated blood."

She nodded. Skip swore and picked up the suitcases. "This way, please," Lasswell said. "My relief has our car parked near here."

It was a Neptune with a civilian number, inconspicuous among a million similar teardrops. The man who scrambled forth was clad like Lasswell but a good deal tougher-looking. "You got 'em!" he cawed.

"Hurry," Lasswell said. "Rear seat, please, Dr. Canter and sir."

He and his companion took the front. "Let me," Skip said, and leaned over to fasten her safety harness. His breath tickled her ear. "Too bad," he whispered. " 'Nother time."

Pilot set, the car hummed into motion. "Better we opaque the windows," Lasswell said, and did.

"Hoy!" Skip exclaimed suddenly. He pointed to a twisted, leathery object suction-clamped on the dashboard. "What's a juju doing in a Secret Service whirr?"

"I can tell you that," Lasswell replied.

He unsnapped his harness and turned around. From beneath his tunic he had drawn a flat gun. Skip snarled and grabbed under his own garments while snatching at his buckle. The gun hissed. Skip jerked, made a rattling noise, rolled back his eyes, and slumped. Horror took Yvonne in a tidal wave. She screamed. The second needle pricked her in the stomach. A jab of cold radiated to hands and feet and head. The wave became a maelstrom and sucked her down into night.

XI

———◆———

Skip woke slowly. Pavement was hard beneath him. His head ached and his mouth tasted foul. The background noise of traffic hurt. He groped through bewilderment. What'd happened? A monumental drunk, a fight, or— Memory slammed back. He sat up with half a yell, half a groan. Lamplight filtered dully around huge pillars whose shadows swamped him. He'd been tucked out of sight beneath an elevated section of railroad.

"Yvonne?" he called weakly. "Yvonne?"

No answer. He climbed to his feet. Dizziness swept through and almost felled him. He stood swaying till it passed, then stumbled out onto the street which crossed under the el. It lay deserted in the dark, warehouses and factories. "Yvonne!" he shouted.

Physical strength and steadiness began returning. Though he had no watch, he recalled that a knockout shot generally put you to sleep for about an hour. He went back behind the pillars, on either side of the street, and hunted for his friend. She wasn't there, of course. The kidnappers only wanted her. They took him for a mere escort and dumped him at the first opportune place, not wishing to be bothered with an extra prisoner.

Get help. Call the police, no, better the FBI.

He started down the sidewalk at random, first shuffling, later striding, finally running as his body threw off the last effects of the drug. The exercise cleared his mind. He found himself thinking with a speed and precision that raised faint surprise at the rear of his brain.

If the object of the game had been to murder Yvonne, like last time, they could have done it, to both, when they stopped to leave him off. A bullet, a slashed throat, a full eight or ten needles, no problem. Therefore they wanted her alive, at any rate until she'd been quizzed by— whoever hired them. For they were obviously local Un-

101

derworlders, topnotch professionals, who knew the scene
and had the organization. He might well have that to
thank for his life. Mercenaries didn't take the risk of
committing murder unless forced by circumstances or unless it was part of the job. In the latter case, the price
went high. Having been told to net Yvonne Canter, they
had done exactly that.

They must be mighty damned confident of their ability
to keep her out of sight, to let Skip give early notice. They
must have foreseen what hounds would be baying after
them. . . . Well, did a few hours make any difference? On
agreeing to the San Clemente jaunt, Yvonne had said she
must call Armstrong and tell them she was okay, or
there'd be a general alarm out before sunrise.

And why should the kidnappers not be confident? They
had the whole megalopolis to choose a lair from. Their
operation had been so smooth in every respect, they
wouldn't have overlooked the details of concealment.

Smooth as a glass ramp going down into hell. The
thought was anguish. His feet thudded, the air tore in and
out of him, gray walls and locked doors fell past, and no
other life stirred, no lighted window appeared; save for
the sky-glow above and the machine throb around, he
might have been the last living creature on Earth.

Knowing the sea gypsies were about due in, a man
could find the exact time by calling the harbormaster's
office. Shadows would be waiting, who would not overlook
the possibility that their quarry might leave by an odd
route. Unsuspecting, untrained in such matters, Skip and
Yvonne would be child's play to follow. In fact, once
they'd checked their luggage, they might not have been
followed at all. It would be ample to post a watcher at the
station.

Secret Service disguise . . . yes, a distinct touch. FBI or
military intelligence credentials were risky to fake, since
Yvonne would often have seen them; her escort might be
equally familiar with local police badges and style; but
how many people ever had anything to do with the Secret
Service?

Who were those men working for? Why kidnap this
time, instead of kill? How had they known she was on
Ormen?

An auto purred by. Skip shouted and waved. The man
inside was watching television and didn't notice. However,
more cars moved on a cross street ahead. This nightmare
race must be near an end. Halting at the corner, lungs

pumping like bellows, spleen aching, mouth and throat dry, skin drenched and stinking, Skip looked around. Neon signs, a cluster of shops and bars, that way!

As he entered a drugstore, fear smote him. He clutched frantically in his pockets. The money was there. His enemies hadn't even considered him worth robbing.

Well, they're right. Tears stung his eyes. *It's my fault. I talked her into visiting Maury—someone must've passed the news in spite of Hightower's request—and I knew in my vast wisdom that she had nothing to fear in this town. If they destroy her, the blood is forever on my hands.*

He located a phone booth and punched for FBI, LA HQ. The screen replicated a man's face. "Federal Bureau of Investigation. William Sleight speaking. May I help you?"

"Better record this," Skip said.

"We routinely do, sir." Impassive, the man kept a disconcertingly steady stare. *I must look wild to him, dusty, sweaty, unkempt.* Skip gathered breath. In a rush of words, while he clenched his fists against the pain of it, he told the story.

Sleight flung questions. At the end, he said, "We'll get right on it. Stay put. We'll send a car. Where are you?"

"You need me? I mean, I'm not inventing this, and I've, I've told you what I know."

"You bet we want you, mister." Sleight had now acquired an expression, as bleak as any Skip had ever seen. "Quick, where are you?" On being told, he nodded, a single downward jerk like an eagle stripping a bone. "Wait inside. At the newsstand. Won't be more than ten minutes." The screen blanked.

Skip left the booth. *You're wrong, buck,* he thought. *It'll be a lot more. They'll lock me up and melt the key.*

Or can they? I'm not guilty of anything, am I? ... Like spit I'm not. . . . Legally guilty, that is. I'm simply a material witness. They can't hold me indefinitely. Can they?

They'll keep me too damn long at best. The vision of walls and warders made him ill. *When I might be doing something to help.*

What might you do, fat boy?

He took a magazine and leafed through it, as a way to occupy hands and eyes. In the immensity of his loneliness, the counters, the clerks, the few customers, the faintly sweet odors, the background music, were unreal, unreachable.

A title appeared, "The Sigman and the Nations." His glance plodded over the page. The author claimed that the governments of Earth were being criminally lax in not making definite, firm advance arrangements for the Peace Authority to control whatever new knowledge and fantastic new technology ought to rush over man when communication with the being from the stars was finally established. Failing this accord, the several delicate equilibriums on which civilization today depended for its survival could be upset. For instance, the Authority's powers of inspection and arrest were confined to certain classes of armaments. The rest were not prohibited, and only a few international regulations—anti-pollution, schedule notification, mutual aid in distress, et cetera—covered spacecraft. But a photon-drive ship was potentially an irresistible weapon. If a great power succeeded in building such a vessel for exclusive use, its rivals would practically be forced to denounce the ban on nuclear warheads, openly or clandestinely; and you didn't need an intercontinental rocket to annihilate a city, you could smuggle your bomb in piecemeal—

Skip raised his head and stared before him. *Sure,* he realized. *That's what this thing tonight is about.*

The Underworld scarcely had a line into Maury. Yet a scientist could be a spy for a government; that had happened often enough in the past. Though Maury did nothing secret, it would be an excellent *pied-à-terre* for an agent assigned to ingratiate himself with men of different nationalities whose work elsewhere did have military significance. He'd sound them out, collecting scraps of information which, fitted together, might at last reveal a hidden truth.

Suppose the Russians, the Chinese, whoever they were—call them X—suppose they'd decided a while back to try getting the jump on others in the Sigman business. Since it wasn't obvious how they could, or whether they could, they'd improvise as they went along. Such absence of doctrine always seemed to open the way for extremists to take charge. When Yvonne made the first crack in the language barrier, she'd revealed herself as the best American on the project. Word must have gone out: "Eliminate her before she develops capabilities that we may not be told about."

Nobody had reason to maintain an expensive and risky organization of his own for work like burglaries and murders, anyhow not in the West. The Underworld was available. You'd hire your assassin deviously—yeah, doubtless tell his ultimate boss that you wanted this research stopped because it was dangerous or blasphemous or Communistic or whatever—

Yvonne escaped, and the U.S. government spirited her away. In the secret councils of Country X, they doubtless wondered if that was strictly for a rest cure. Or if it was, mightn't she have a fresh inspiration during her holiday? So . . . kidnap her if possible and wring out what she knew before disposing of her existence. When X's agent in Maury saw Yvonne and learned where she would debark, he must have sneaked a phone call to his American contact. (Maybe he himself didn't suspect his masters were after her. His job could simply be to inform them of everything interesting that came to his attention.) X's local man was notified in turn, and promptly hired men from the Angeleno torpedo guild, and the rest followed.

Skip flinched. The inevitability was crushing. In an hour under babble juice, quizzed by a skilled operator, Yvonne would pass on the whole of what she and he had developed. The operator would curse that his superiors hadn't thought to instruct that any companion of hers be included in the package. *They'll try for me. But I'll be safely in jail.* She would be useless, yes, hazardous to keep. The operator would turn her back to the professionals for elimination.

They might well amuse themselves with her a while before they let her die.

Unless she's dead already— No, I mustn't think that. And they, X, must need time to prepare. They got short notice and they can't have a big, permanently alerted, Underworld-style outfit in this country. I imagine their quizmaster'll have to be flown here from home. And smuggling him in is taking an unnecessary chance, so a cover must first be arranged for him. And matters will have to be fixed at this end so the torpedoes won't guess who they've really been working for.

Still, a day or two at most. And the FBI must have leads to the Underworld, but the Feds are limited in what they can do and they've got this whole monster of a supercity to cover—

Skip dropped the magazine. *Judas on a stick!* I *can do things!*

A mature man would have stayed and offered his advice and services to the authorities. But that would take hours,

at the end of which his idea might be dismissed. Besides,
Skip had never claimed to be mature. A wall clock said
his ten minutes were nearly gone. He left the store in a
rush. "Hey, taxi!" Only later did it occur to him that he
should have called in and reported his theory about the
Sigman, lest it die in America with him and Yvonne.

The One of the Los Angeles area was male and called
himself Elohath. His dwelling was in a slum district and
from the outside seemed to be another rotting centenarian
of a house, grotesquely turreted, bayed, scrimshawed, and
scaly-shingled, in a yard rank with weeds and trash. Skip
dismissed his cab two blocks away and proceeded on foot.
Nobody else seemed to be abroad. What windows were
lighted had the blinds drawn; none could be opaqued.
Infrequent, antiquated incandescent street lamps stood
goblinlike in puddles of dingy luminance. Above the background mutter of megalopolis, a palm tree rubbed fronds
together in the rapidly chilling breeze, a skeletal sound.
Sheets of paper scrittled across the walk. A cat slunk
under a hedge reverting to brush.

Skip mounted the porch and pressed the doorbell, a
further anachronism. He hoped he wouldn't be left here
long, among ugly pillars silhoutted against a dull red
sky-glow. *Brrrr!* sounded through the heavy old door.
Brrrr! Brrrr!

It opened. A woman in a black robe, who would have
been good-looking if less hard-faced and if every hair had
not been removed from her head, asked, "What is your
desire?"

"I have to see the One," Skip answered. "Right away.
No, I don't have an appointment. It's terribly urgent,
though."

She considered. Elohath must get scores of callers a
year who were weird even by his lights. Skip tried to look
his youngest and most clean-cut. "Come in, please, and we
will discuss it," she said at length.

When the door had closed behing him, Skip was in
richness. Drapes of purple velvet screened the rooms that
gave on the dark-paneled corridor down which he was
guided. Bulbs in ornate, seven-branched brackets provided
dim vision. The black rug deadened sound, so thick and
soft that it felt alive beneath his feet. From somewhere,
just audible, wailed a minor-key chant.

Reaching an antechamber, the woman took a seat behind a huge desk. Phone and intercom were housed in a

case carven with demonic faces, on top of which rested a human skull. Walls and ceiling were hung with red and black cloth. The floor was as luxuriously covered as in the hallway. A slightly bitter incense swirled from a brazier. Above an inner door was a Tetragrammaton.

Elohath's a better than average charlatan, Skip reflected. *But then, he'd better be. He isn't fleecing ordinary sheep.* (*How did it happen, superstition making the comeback it's done? Already in Dad's childhood, educated people were solemnly using astrology. Could science maybe be too demanding?—Anyway, in superstitiousness I suppose the criminal classes have always taken first prize.*) *Among Elohath's clientele are the barons of the Angeleno Underworld. If they ever stopped fearing him, he'd be done; he knows too much.*

"Be seated." The woman pointed to a chair. Skip obeyed. She took a printed form from a drawer. "I'll need certain information before I can decide whether to disturb the One on your account. Last night he had to raise a dead man, and frankly, that leaves him tired for days afterward."

"He's met me," Skip said. "Bats Bleadon was showing me around a couple of years ago. We attended a séance here and I was introduced. The One very kindly had an acolyte give me a tour of the unforbidden parts of the mansion."

"Indeed?" Her bleached-white countenance registered more interest. "That was before my time. May I have your name?"

Skip gave it. She punched for the data file; Elohath was not above using electronic storage and retrieval. Reading the screen, she nodded. "Ah, yes. Mr. Bleadon spoke highly of you. Why haven't you been around since?"

"I left town for, hm, various reasons. Didn't come back till yesterday." Skip was not play-acting the desperation in his voice: "Please, Darkangel! I've got to see the One right away! The business could touch him as well as Bats— No, I can't tell you what. You don't want to know, believe me, Darkangel. Look, if he gets mad, he can take it out on me, not you."

"I shall inquire," she said, and pushed the intercom switch. After a short conversation, she finished, "My thanks to my Lord," cut circuit, and told Skip: "You may enter in seven minutes. Meanwhile be silent and compose your thoughts."

How'm I gonna do that last? The woman stared blank-

eyed before her. Elohath's secretaries got rigorous training, all right. As for the boss, he'd doubtless been relaxing
in his private quarters—*not necessarily with a succubus or
an occult tome; why not the Downey Clown Show, if he's
alone?*—and needed time to put his costume back on.

A husky shavepate whose robe wouldn't hamper him in
a fight entered when the secretary rang. "You realize
weapons may not be borne in the sanctum," he said.
"Please stand and hold out your arms." He patted Skip
efficiently. "Very well. Thank you."

If he'd discovered the fang, Skip would have been in
deep trouble. But it was inside an elastic waistband which
forced it to match the curvature of the wearer's body. The
slight extra bulge and hardness were scarcely detectable
against his muscular abdomen.

"Remember to halt three paces from the throne, bow
three times with thumbs crossed on breast, and wait to
speak until you are spoken to," the secretary said while
the guard demonstrated. "You may go in now."

Skip's pulse racketed in his ears. The sweat was chill
where it trickled from armpits down ribs. His tongue felt
like a block of wood. Somehow he opened the door,
walked through, and closed it behind him. Its massiveness
and the hiss when it settled back in the frame bespoke
soundproofing.

Alone in a short, gloomy corridor, he unsnapped the
pocket in his waistband and drew out the fang. It was a
thin, slowly straightening brown ribbon, 30 centimeters
long, four centimeters wide, two millimeters thick. He
rapped it sharply against a shoe. Jarred, the plastic sprang
back to the original shape it "remembered." He felt an
instant's expansion and snaky writhing, and held a knife
with a ten-centimeter blade. The inset edge and point,
around which the ribbon had been folded, gleamed razor-
keen.

Restoring the former configuration would take longer.
He'd heat the plastic till its present rigidity became
softness, force it into a "mold" he carried in his pack, and
restow it. Otherwise, unconstrained, it would soon become
a knife again. His slap had merely hastened that. For the
present, he tucked it between pants and underwear, letting
his tunic fall concealingly over. The whole job had taken a
few seconds. In a pinch he could do it much faster.

Sometimes he wondered how long it would be until the
idea was blown or reinvented and spread. Meanwhile,

Hank Sunshine, who made the things, gave them only to sigaroons he trusted.

Feeling a little more self-confident, Skip went on down the hall and through the door to the room beyond.

It was in the same style as the antechamber, but huge in extent and height. The windows were draped; shadows dwelt thick between the few wan lights. Shelves of musty leather-bound books dominated two walls, a rack of magical and alchemical apparatus a third. Showcases holding curious objects—he noticed a thighbone, a caul, and a mummified fetus among them—flanked the entrance. A crimson carpet laid over the black marked his way to the throne.

He trod the path, which seemed to stretch on and on, and made his obeisance. "By our Father God, our Mother Ashtoreth, and the legions of the Otherworld: my son, be welcome," said the rustling voice above him. "Peace upon those who come hither in reverence. Speak freely and unafraid, save that you must be brief, for you are not the single troubled soul who has need of my succor."

Skip looked up. Elohath seemed tall in his midnight robe. Its cowl surrounded a face white as the woman's, gaunt as this house. About his neck hung the ancient fig symbol. The cross on the rosary at his waist had a crescent for arms. In his right hand, like a scepter, he held a crooked staff.

Suddenly Skip lost nervousness. He saw, heard, smelled, felt more sharply than he could remember from aforetime. His thoughts sprang forward in disciplined ranks. Underneath was a rage so driving, so powerful that it was as if a demon had truly possessed him.

"Lord," he began, "what I've got to tell is ... well, you better read my mind or you'll call me a liar."

"Let me first hear you, my son."

"But—pardon me, Lord, but do make sure nobody is listening, like on an intercom. We can't trust— Well, what I'm here about is trouble with the heavies. The Feds."

"The government knows me as a licensed minister and counselor." Elohath's tone had gone a shade less calm. The fraudulence of years was too strong for him not to add: "If I told you the names of certain clients— Proceed."

Yeh, yeh, yeh, gibed at the back of Skip's head. *And you give your well-paid advice after you've read the future in the stars or an inkpool or your navel or wher-*

*ever; you cast spells; you exercise clairvoyance; you sell
amulets, charms, philtres; you bless, you curse, you put on
a damnably good show; you must've mastered every trick
that every magician, illusionist, fortune teller, medium,
telepath, you-name-it has ever worked out for spooking
his fellow men into awe and generosity.*

Most of him was gauging distance and layout. The
chamber might be continuously monitored by guards—but
probably not, for many secrets were confided to the One
and a guard might be bribable or kidnappable. Elohath
would have an alarm button in the chair or someplace.
However, since his visitors were supposed to be unarmed
and he had that heavy staff and perhaps a gun, he
wouldn't really be worried about assault—not that those
who came to this Endor, in fear or greed or hatred or
grief, would dare offend the summoner of angels, fiends,
ghosts. . . .

He was leaning forward, tense, free hand on a knee. No
better chance to take him was likely to come.

Skip made the distance in two jumps. On the second, he
twisted in midair. His left foot preceded him, a karate
kick to the solar plexus. The throne went over backward
with a rug-muffled thud. Skip hit the dais and rolled to the
floor. He bounced directly up, drew his knife, and sprang
to his victim. The One lay limp. *Hey, the old bastard's not
dead, is he?* Skip's dismay was at the chance that his sole
line to Yvonne would be cut. No, breath wheezed, Elohath was just stunned. Skip straightened the throne. In
case somebody looked in, that'd be an item less to explain
away. He carried the other to a couch in the farthest,
darkest corner of the room, laid him down, and checked
for weapons. None; this fellow *was* well in the saddle.

The One stirred and groaned. "Okay, chum, come out
of it," Skip said. He slapped a cheek. Elohath's eyelids
fluttered. He clutched his belly and retched. Skip showed
him the blade. "I want information, you. I want it fast
and I want it accurate."

"What—" Elohath struggled to a sitting position. He
began tracing signs and mouthing noises.

Skip slapped him again. "Save your show. Maybe
you've cursed a few people to their doom because they
believed in it and wasted away. I'm not about to. Listen.
If we're interrupted, you tell the person we're in conference and he's to leave us be. At the first sign of anything I
can't handle, I'll kill you. To make that plausible, let me
point out that I'll have nothing to lose. I know quite well

what your goons would do to me. So after your heart's skewered, mine comes next. Cooperate and you won't be hurt."

"What do you want?" Elohath whispered.

Skip related the kidnapping, not only describing the two operatives but exhibiting drawings he had made en route in his ever-present notepad. "I know your system," he finished. "Besides the usual hokum, it depends on an intelligence network most professional spies would envy. Clients tell you things; you keep runners out, observers, snoopers, collators, information exchange with colleagues elsewhere. The heavies would give their left kidneys to know what you know, which is why you're careful never to lend them an excuse for arresting you."

"I . . . am . . . a law-abiding citizen. You—"

"I am a felon of the worst kind," Skip said, more cheerfully than he felt. "I want to learn where these two horns are, who they're affiliated with, where they're probably denned, any alternative spots, what kind of guards and other security they may have—the whole shebang, Elohath."

"Privileged information," the One said. He had his wind back, and his cunning and ratlike courage.

"Yeah, you'll be shot slowly if it's ever found out you betrayed a client. It doesn't have to be found out, if we arrange this right. You'll for sure be dead if you don't talk to me. Now!"

"No! Azreal, destroy him! Semphoragas, ya lamiel—" The invocation was cut off by an arm around the throat.

Skip hated the next few minutes. That what he was doing left no marks made it somehow worse. Only the thought of Yvonne in captivity kept him active. Elohath was getting on in years, physically not strong. He broke. "Yes, yes, I'll talk, damn you, you devil, damn you—"

"Begin," Skip said into the sobbing.

By the time Elohath had spoken what he recalled offhand, he had recovered sufficiently to use the intercom. A considerable file was duplicated at his behest on the ReaderFax behind a screen. "We'll want to protect you," Skip said after going through it, "so you'll have a motive for not blowing the whistle on me. Is yonder phone a relay job?"

Elohath nodded miserably. Skip had expected as much. Elsewhere in the city was an instrument through which messages to and from this one traveled. A continuously operating scanner would reveal if strangers came into that distant room after having presumably traced a call. The connection to here would immediately be broken and a new line arranged for.

Skip made his prisoner lie on the floor, under his foot, and rang up the FBI. Sleight was still at the desk. "You!" he exploded. "What—"

"I think I've found where Dr. Canter is," Skip said brusquely. He gave names, addresses, and pertinent details. "That's in order of likelihood. I'd suggest sleep-gas bombs before the men go in, but you know more about that than I do. And blood of Christ, man, *hurry!*"

"Where do you get this stuff?" Sleight demanded. "How do we know you're telling the truth?"

"Dare you assume I'm not? I'll call back in an hour." Skip cut circuit and released the One.

"We can spend the time planning," he said. "You see, if I told them how I came by my information, I'd be confessing to a serious crime. I might get probation, but the whole thing'd be tedious and messy, I'd have a bad mark on my record, I'd be denied clearance to work with Dr. Canter—you can write the scenario yourself. Therefore you and I have the same interest in kitty-littering the truth."

Elohath stared long at him. "You're as sharp as you're tough," he murmured. "If you're ever interested in a job—"

"*¿Quien sabe?* Far's that goes, you rascal, if I can ever do you a favor that's not too flinkin' unethical, you might ask. Now let's concoct."

Between Skip's imagination and the One's knowledge, a tale was worked out that ought to serve. Skip had sought former Underworld acquaintances in the hope of getting a lead. Among them was a man who, by sheer good fortune, happened to be a disgruntled, recently expelled member of the same mercenary outfit that had snatched Yvonne. (He was real, well-known to the police. Nothing except the fact that, three nights earlier, he had gone down the garbage grinder of a rival, need be withheld.) Skip had drawn him out, aided by his natural resentment and a large supply of pot.

After this was settled, Elohath and guest chatted, not entirely unamicably. Beneath his lightness, Skip's tension approached breaking point. It was with shaking fingers that he punched the FBI number at hour's end.

"Yes, we have her," Sleight said. "Locked in a room at the first house you listed, scared and shocked but otherwise unharmed. Unfortunately, the men we took with her don't seem to have known more than that they were supposed to stand by for further orders. A couple escaped. They were in the rear of the house, with access to a tunnel our boys found afterward. Hence no point in trying to set a trap. *Now* will you come here?"

"I'm on my way." Skip switched off and spent a while breathing. Finally: "I'm sorry to inconvenience you further, old boy. However, you realize I must protect my line of retreat."

"Certainly." Elohath pressed the intercom. "Darkangel Zaaphyra, Mr. Wayburn is leaving. I want to be left strictly alone to meditate upon his news." Skip bound him with strips cut from the curtains, in a set of ties that an escape artist would take about half an hour to work free of. It wouldn't do for a One to be found trussed like a hog. Having gagged him, Skip patted him on the head and departed.

"Be seated, Comrade Professor," General Chou said. Wang Li took the chair at which the cigarette pointed. There followed a minute's quiet. Finally, from behind a veil of smoke, Chou stated:

"You should know, because she may mention it to you, a second attempt has been made on Yvonne Canter."

"No!" A part of Wang observed that he sounded almost as appalled as he was. "I have not heard—"

"You would not have. The American authorities are suppressing the facts, thus far at any rate. We know because we have agents among them: which is not a wicked thing, Comrade Professor, when they would like to do the same to us and have possibly succeeded."

"I understand," Wang said low. "Was she hurt?"

"No. This was a kidnapping, by hired criminals. The fascist police recovered her and took a few prisoners who knew nothing of value. Apart from this: that in her fright and confusion she had babbled to them about a fresh concept of the Sigman, something which would open the way to a real alliance. She evidently hoped they would free her on that account. Upon seeing their indifference, she spoke no further."

"Who can have been responsible?" Wang made himself ask.

"Who knows?" Chou replied. "The Soviets, the Japanese, the West Europeans—or it could have been engineered by the American regime itself, hiring real gangsters but meaning to sacrifice them in a show for the purpose of frightening her into total conformity." He leaned across his desk. "Consider this, Professor Wang. The incident occurred days ago. Dr. Canter must have recovered and told her great idea to her superiors. Every discovery about the Sigman is supposed to be promptly shared. We have received no word about this latest. What does that indicate to you?"

"They may be unsure," Wang faltered. "They may have decided she was mistaken."

"Or they may be stealing a march on us," Chou snapped. "We are preparing against that. I called you here in order that you shall, for every contingency we can imagine, know what is your duty."

XII

To his surprise, Skip found Andrew Almeida a likable man, generally relaxed and easygoing, talkative but a good listener, holder of a master's degree in history, sensitive appreciator of the arts, head of a charming family whose hospitality was large and unfeigned on weekends in their mountain cabin.

That was about the sole leisure Skip got. For the rest, he had a room on base, and when he wasn't conferring he was being trained. He must learn the results of three years of Sigman studies, get them into his bones, for if his scheme worked there was no predicting what the creature would do and his reaction in turn ought not to be blind. Well, that was whoopee by him. He didn't even mind the celibacy, much. When he was taken into Earth orbit to learn the rudiments of free-fall coordination—when he saw, no simulacrum between walls, the Mother Herself before his eyes, shining among the stars—it was the lordliest hour of his life thus far.

Meanwhile the FBI must be trying to check out his past. He leered and wished them joy. Yvonne's influence had gotten him a temporary clearance which sufficed.

After a month, Almeida's final briefing came as a blow.

He sat behind the desk in his office, Skip and Yvonne in chairs facing him. A window stood open to cool air, to rumble and bustle, to buildings across the way and beyond them a glimpse of the steeplelike rocket which tomorrow dawn would lift on flame and pierce blue heaven.

Almeida stuffed his pipe. "I wish we could have spent more time preparing for this mission," he said.

Yvonne drew on a cigarette. Though she looked tense and jittery, Skip admired the aquiline profile, tilted eyes, lustrous hair, figure damn good, really, beneath her severe business dress, in a lean long-legged fashion. . . . "We're

115

about as ready as we can be," she said. "If we dawdle, the Sigman may leave on a new junket, or for home."

"Right," the colonel agreed. "Or somebody may independently come on Skip's notion."

Yvonne straightened in her chair. "Andy," she said, "I don't like the way we've been hugging the concept to us. Among other reasons, I want to discuss it with my foreign associates, Duclos in particular. He's bound to have valuable thoughts, being a connoisseur in private life. I obeyed you hitherto because we were busy explaining and laying detailed plans. But I don't want to keep silence any longer."

Skip tugged an earlobe. "Uh, I figured the secrecy wasn't too bad a notion, Yvonne," he ventured. "After what happened to you and— Shouldn't we have stopped to think before bulling ahead on something this important? If we were wrong, we've only stalled progress a month. Because how can we hide our doings after we've gone aboard?"

"That," said Almeida, "is what I aim to discuss today."

His lighter popped into flame, an unexpectedly loud noise. Yvonne started. Skip touched a hand to the fang he had not seen fit to mention here either.

Almeida developed a good head of steam before he leaned elbows on desk and said with unwonted gravity: "We've informed the appropriate agencies abroad that we're sending a boat there tomorrow. They keep radar surveillance the same as us. But we've claimed it's a routine check on the outer fringes of the Sigman's force-field, to see if there've been any changes. There never have been, you know, but it's sensible to reinvestigate periodically; and the maneuvers are good practice for astronauts. Nobody else cared to come along, as we expected.

"You will orbit close and transmit your program on the original Sigman waveband, holding power too low for detection more than a few kilometers off. That way, if you get a response, the fact can be kept confidential."

"Huh?" Skip exclaimed. "Now wait just one mucking minute."

Almeida lifted a hand. "You needn't tell me. A dirty trick, a violation of solemn covenants. But suppose the Sigman's response is a complete set of plans for its ship. Not fantastic. We're obviously a race interested in technology. Or something less foreseeable may happen." The hand became a fist and smote the desktop. *"We don't know.* And we don't have solid, enforceable international agreements concerning these things. You needn't blame Chinese intransigence or American paranoia or whatever your pet whipping boy is. Simply consider the problem in preparing for events that can't really be imagined, let alone predicted. And the more players there are in a game, the less stable the game becomes."

He sighed. "Maybe, if you establish meaningful communication, you should ask the Sigman to go away till the human race has grown up," he said. "Or maybe, and I hope this is most likely, the knowledge will prove safe enough, introduced gradually enough, that we can return to wide-open operations. For the present, however, we fight a delaying action."

Yvonne's lips trembled. She dabbed at her eyes.

"What if the Sigman invites us to tea?" Skip asked. "We've been kind of assuming it'll do so, if our scheme works. Manned satellites are always watching for that rainbow come-on."

"Maybe you can somehow make it omit the signal," Almeida suggested. "Or, having boarded, maybe you can persuade it to close the forcefield again. In such a case, we'll fob off indignant protests by claiming that evidently a misunderstanding occurred. . . . Responsibility doesn't rest entirely on your shoulders. Your pilot and copilot were carefully picked. Major Thewlis has had combat experience—the Rock incident, for example. Captain Kurland is with Air Force intelligence. Let me make plain the ground rules under which you'll operate."

Skip was lost in contemplation of the spacecraft. That gladsome dance of mass and shape, where sun and shadow lilted, was like Earth afloat in the universe, like music, like love and adventure and creating—you could only experience it by experiencing it. The words of the finest writers, the pictures of the finest holographic photographers, had never suggested what sacredness was here.

This spearhead, that curve, yonder spiral, yes, I see how they flow together to make oneness and rise back renewed.

Kurland tapped him on the shoulder. "We're in orbit, Mr. Wayburn."

Jarred from his trance, Skip bounced against his harness. The cabin crowded him with instruments, the air smelled stale, a pump was whickering, weightlessness was pleasant but he knew how it would hamper his unskilled muscles, the window through which he had gazed was small and smeared. "Oh. Oh, yeah," he mumbled stupidly.

"Can you get busy right away?" Thewlis asked.

"Yes, of course." Yvonne began unfastening.

"Remember," Kurland told Skip, "from time to time we'll have to snort, correcting for drift, if we want to maintain our relative position. Won't be more than a tenth of a gee at the outside, and we'll warn you in advance."

Skip's nod was impatient. Returned to full awareness, he was ablaze with his mission. If it was victorious, what glories might he not see! Releasing himself, he bobbed across the cabin toward the visiphone transmitter, where he clipped on a tether and started unpacking the objects brought along.

Yvonne helped. Her voice was troubled: "I could almost wish we draw blank." She tossed her head. "No, I don't!"

"If we do," Skip said needlessly, "we'll keep trying."

"How do you know the Sigman receiver is on?" Kurland asked behind him.

"We don't," Thewlis said. "But wouldn't you leave yours on, recording, and check the tapes at intervals?"

"My guess is, a monitoring gadget is set to holler when something comes in that looks like pay dirt," Skip said. "Oops! Damn!" A wad of cotton, padding for a bowl, escaped him.

Thewlis fielded it. "I still don't understand what basis you picked your specimens on," he remarked.

"Guesswork, mostly," Skip confessed, "We needed a wide variety. However, since this boat can't carry a British Museumful, we made low bulkiness one criterion. And we chose the majority of exhibits from what we thought was likeliest to appeal. I can't explain our method. We'd try to abstract Sigman conventions from what humans have seen of the ship, and reason from there. Speaking honest, though: it was a lot more hunch and intuition than logic."

"Mostly Skip's," Yvonne added. "That's how I got him cleared. Checkered background or no, I said, who else had a better chance of succeeding?"

An hour later, the duplicated masterpieces racked in order, the script of the show clipboarded before them, he and she looked at each other and clasped hands. He saw how the pulse fluttered in her throat. His own mouth was dry. *Quick, what can I say at this historic moment? The Eagle has laid an egg— No, hell, let's just slog ahead.* He activated the visual scanner. Yvonne began to speak on the synthesizer.

"*Humans ... approach ... Sigman. Humans ... approach . . . Sigman. Human-Sigman. Human-Sigman.*" Presently she nodded to Skip. The screen before them remained blank, but he lifted the first of his choices, a Mondrian pattern. He didn't think the alien would find its subtle simplicity more than mildly interesting, but it could lead the way to photographs of a Japanese torii gate, Chinese calligraphy—

—Dürer, Michelangelo, Velasquez, Rembrandt, Corot, Motonobu, Lung-Mien, Persian miniatures and Lascaux bison whose creators were forgotten but never, never the work—

—the curve of a Hindu cup or a Grecian vase, the virility of a Polynesian war club or an African mask, the sinister grace of an Aztec skull carved in crystal, the serene charm of a Russian icon carved in wood—

—pictures of larger sculptures, Nefertiti's head, Aphrodite and Nike, but here chiefly the more recent masters, Rodin, Brancusi, Milles, Nielsen—of parks and gardens—of the noblest and the most charming houses men had raised, temples, palaces, cottages, bowers, castles, tombs—

For this had been the artist's insight: that the traveler had made its lonely pilgrimage because it too was an artist, in search of nothing less than beauty.

"Hey!" shouted Thewlis. "It's lit! Like a goddamn Christmas tree!"

Skip twisted wildly about. From his post he could glimpse an edge of the Sigman vessel, kilometers distant. No longer did the space between look empty. It flamed with colors, all colors, from the deep pure fluorescences to the softest tints a sunrise or a flower might blend, whirling and flickering and twining, till it was as if the watcher became part of their ecstasy and went beyond this whole cosmos.

Kurland's voice drew him back: "Jee-*zus*, but you got through. The invitation's never been half that bright or lively before, am I right?"

"You are," said Thewlis. Hushed: "They haven't made words for this."

"Maybe the Sigmans have," Kurland said out of the same wonder.

Yvonne broke into tears.

Thewlis shook himself and turned from the spectacle. "Well, our hope of maintaining complete secrecy always was faint," he said tonelessly. "The big thing is, we've made contact—you two have—and now we go by Plan Charlie." He unbuckled. "I'll help you load your stuff. We can stick those things right in the rack and tow them over, correct?"

"I'll break out the spacesuits and gear," Kurland stated.

The auroral marvel outside was lost in a scramble of preparation.

"Okay," Thewlis said before closing his faceplate. "Let's review procedure a final time. We'll stand by as usual. Once aboard, you do what seems best. If you possibly can, get the Sigman to shut the entryway behind you. Then spend the rest of your time there convincing it to communicate only with Americans. I know what a tall order that is, especially when you've got perhaps thirty hours before the foreign ships start arriving."

"Maybe less," Kurland said. "We know they've kept standbys on about one-day countdowns since you brought the big news, Dr. Canter. But somebody could have a surprise in reserve."

Yvonne winced. "I'll be so embarrassed, so ashamed, if—"

Kurland clapped her on the armored shoulder. The force drove her a ways from him. "Have you forgotten your cover story?" he asked. "Skip's idea seemed too wild to broach officially, but as long as he, a recruit, needed training, we figured on our low level, not bothering to notify Washington, we might as well give it a whirl. You came along for the ride and on the off chance. Nobody was more flabbergasted than us when it paid off."

Yvonne's face was lost and unhappy in her helmet. "I'm not a good liar," she said. "I hate lying."

"I'm an expert," Skip assured her, "and outside of my friends, I enjoying practicing the trade. Shall we go?"

Wang Li arrived within ten hours.

Skip and Yvonne had lost track of the world, had forgotten about him. There, in that curving chamber, confronting that dome where elven forms and leaves and blooms crowded the air, they were coming to know one who fared between the stars.

"What most of the lattice and all of the plants are," Skip breathed. "I'll bet my right index finger. Not machinery, not oxygen renewal; the ship must have more effective systems. But pleasure. Renewal of the spirit."

Yvonne regarded the great, dripping, rugged shape be-

yond. By now, every showpiece had been passed through
the curious portal. The Sigman floated, rapt in a photograph of York Minster's Five Sisters. "Do you know," she
said as softly, "it isn't hideous. Not by our standards
either, when you look at it right."

"Shucks, I could'a told them that three years back,"
Skip answered.

Across his mind drifted recollection of what he had said
to her, their first day alone on the sea ship: "Because
most people lack the taste to realize the Sigman is not
repulsive, I suppose unconsciously they took for granted
it's a philistine. Sure, plenty of thinkers figured it'd be
interested in our art, same's we'd be in Sigman art—but
from the outside, as another phenomenon to observe and
write a scientific paper about. What art they showed it at
the beginning was such a small proportion of the diagrams
and whatnot, and damn near randomly chosen, our chum
may not even have recognized the objects for what they
were. And anyway, priority was put on communication by
words. Everybody assumed that when that'd been
achieved, any further matters could be discussed at leisure. They forgot words are by no means the only language. It never occurred to them the Sigman might've
made this tremendous voyage for *no* other purpose than
artistic inspiration—that the planets themselves provided
so much that it begrudged what time it gave us, seeing as
how we never brought anything it particularly wanted—"

His reminiscence broke off. The Sigman was ap-
proaching the dome wall. The photograph was held lightly
in one set of claws. The surrounding tentacle-fingers had
plucked, from a resting place between vines, an album on
the Parthenon. Another "hand" gripped the optical projector.

Skip moved close. Awkward, he cartwheeled and swore.
His inexperience in free fall kept delaying matters. Finally
he got himself braced, sketchpad and pencil ready. Holographic equipment had been brought along but didn't
seem indicated at the moment. The Sigman pointed at the
pictures while tracing lines of light which remained aglow
until it erased or altered them. Skip's pencil flew in response.

"Uh-huh," he said, mainly thinking aloud, "it's fas-
cinated by the contrast between Classical and Perpendicu-
lar architecture . . . is my guess. What do they have in
common? Well, like the Golden Rectangle—I s'pose I can
make that clear—" He remembered his companion. "Say,

Yvonne, here's a chance to extend the verbal language a bit, if I can convey an offer to swap sketches for its learning words—"

A spacesuited figure flew in. "Oh!" Yvonne half screamed. Skip spoke more pungently.

Wang Li checked his trajectory, secured baggage, and opened helmet. Cold fury congealed his features. "What is this?" he demanded. A forefinger stabbed at Skip.

The sigaroon bristled. "Sir, the proper pronoun is 'who.' Or if you mean your question literally, then it's my belly button."

Yvonne floated, gulping. "You ... Professor Wang ... th-th-this soon?" she stammered.

The Chinese glared. "My service insured itself against treachery. I had hoped the precautions were needless."

"But—no, no—"

"I assume you do not intend murder," Wang said. "I shall inform my escorting officer that he can return to our ship." He left.

Skip sought Yvonne, to hold and comfort her. The effort was a fiasco; he ended floundering in midair while his sketchbook and pencil drifted from reach. She remained alone in her desolation. The Sigman hooted. "Sorry 'bout this," Skip muttered at it.

Wang returned and started removing his spacesuit. Skip drifted within reach of a handgrip and stopped himself. He needed a minute to recover from the dizziness raised by centrifugal and Coriolis forces before he could say: "Let me introduce myself. I'm Thomas Wayburn. You must be the Wang Li I've heard tell of. Honored to know you." *Like the buck who got tarred and feathered and ridden out of town on a rail, and when they asked him later how he felt about it, he said that except for the honor, he'd sooner not have.* "I'm a new recruit who seems to've touched off the most surprising development in this project since—"

"Yes, you have a glib story prepared," Wang said. "Please spare me. What are those objects in the dome? Pictures and— This was no deed of impulse. What is your plot?"

Skip was spared an immediate need to reply by the Sigman's vanishing aft. Yvonne rallied and said, "Just when we had kindled interest there, yes, eagerness, you interrupted."

Wang pinched his mouth together. He continued unsuiting and making his living arrangements. Skip thought:

This kicks us over to Plan Delta. Though I doubt we'll find a chance to hoodwink him, if he's the shrewdie they say. Odds are we'll be driven back to perfect honesty and straightforwardness. Well, that's more relaxing—

There was no sound, no shiver. Suddenly they, everything loose . . . drifted to the dome surface, a slow and gentle descent, yes, descent, because "up" and "down" existed again . . . weight increased minute by minute, and Wang cried aloud in Chinese, Yvonne gasped, Skip yelled, "We're moving!"

Wang's lean form straightened. "Quickly," he rapped. "Too many articles have been placed in the expectation of continued weightlessness. We must rearrange them before they topple together and are ruined."

Skip respected him for that; and the job did take his mind off itself. Not that he was afraid. The Sigman could ream the humans out by better means than this, if it wanted. Excitement trumpeted in him. *Where are we bound?* Still, the prosaic tasks of straightening out the mess helped him stay on a moderately even keel. By the time they were finished, acceleration had stabilized at what Wang and Yvonne agreed must be the one-third gee normally observed. Skip reveled in bounding around, feathery-light, till she begged him to stop.

"Not now. We have to think. What are we going to do?"

"Why, wait till our host returns," Skip said. "You knows a better 'ole?—And here he is."

The Sigman clambered stolidly about the lattice, assembling the artwork. Yvonne shook her head. "My ears hurt," she complained.

"Mine likewise," Wang said. "And do we not appear to be speaking more loudly?"

The reason burst upon Skip. "Chew and swallow," he advised. "Equalize air pressure inside and out. Pressure's rising. I'll bet you, Professor Wang, I'll bet you a dinner at the best restaurant in Peking against a can of slumgullion, it'll reach about two Earth atmospheres and stop. We can stand that and the Sigman probably requires it." He hugged Yvonne. His laughter came half gleeful, half hysterical. "It wants us to come join it!"

XIII

Surely never before had children of Adam made so strange a journey this side of death.

For a timeless time that watches and calendars finally counted as seven weeks, the great ship swung around the Solar System. It did not seek the outermost reaches. That would have taken much longer, across the unimaginable vastness of this least lost eddy near the rim of the galactic whirlpool. But speed, mounting instant by instant (at a rate which turned out to be an order of magnitude lower than what that fantastic engine was capable of), carried it a hundred million kilometers from a standing start in seventy hours. The next equal period saw thrice as much distance added; and thus the faring went. Using the second half of the transit from world to world for braking, interplanetary passages were still reckoned in days.

Nor were the interludes of travel empty. For Skip in particular, every waking minute overflowed with discovery and achievement. Sheer physical exhaustion would send him toppling into a sleep which was almost a faint; but he awoke refreshed, ravenous less for food than for more work, more rapture.

Practical problems had early been taken care of. "I trust the Sigman realizes our food supply is limited," Yvonne said.

"Let us eat in its presence and pantomime," Wang suggested.

"No, let me draw pictures," Skip countered. "We're catching on to each other's graphic idioms already. Main problem is, it's used to three-dimensional representation—kind of an X-ray view to boot, like some aboriginal human styles—but I can prob'ly borrow the optical projector, and anyhow I know it savvies perspective on a flat surface, because when I render cubes and such that way, it copies them off three-D, and vice versa."

Wang registered irritation. He plainly didn't like chatter.

The Sigman soon understood, or rather had foreseen the problem. It took them to a place where an enigmatic quicksilvery shape hummed, and made gestures. A bar of brownish material slid forth onto a tray (?). Skip and the Sigman exchanged sketches. "People-type food," he reported.

"How can it be certain?" Yvonne fretted. "I'm convinced it means well. But this stuff could be 99 percent nourishing to us and one percent deadly poison. We're none of us an analytical chemist, even if the equipment were aboard."

Skip shrugged. "Reckon we need a guinea pig."

Glance met glance and recoiled. Wang said slowly, "I do not wish to seem coldblooded, but Mr. Wayburn is untrained, the most nearly expendable."

"No!" Yvonne seized Skip's wrist. Her tone was frantic. "He's the one we can't do without. The artist, the— You or I, Wang Li!"

"Uh-uh." Skip shook his head. "Not you, robin. How 'bout we toss a coin, Professor?"

"And I lose, and die, and two Americans remain?" Wang spoke quietly. His face was less hostile than it was set. But he stood immovable. "Never."

The moment stretched—until Yvonne grabbed the bar, bit off a piece, and swallowed.

Skip caught her to him. "You all right?" Across her shoulder he spat at Wang, "You son of a bitch."

"No, stop, don't fight," Yvonne pleaded. "I'm not hurt. The thing's delicious. Like, oh, steak and Gravenstein apples? I'm going to finish it and you two are going to shake hands."

Tension did not depart from beneath the surface of politeness for an Earth-day. Then, when she reported herself in excellent health, the three of them started learning from the Sigman how to use the machine.

Was "machine" right? Like almost everything they encountered, the apparatus had no mechanical controls, perhaps no moving parts whatsoever. You waved your hands in a certain area, in certain patterns, guided by displays which appeared before your eyes. Reading those was not hard. Thus you determined the kind, amount, and temperature of what would be produced (presumably from waste matter, conceivably reassembled atom by atom in a set of hydromagnetic fields). Nothing that came out was distasteful or dangerous. After a while, when communication was better, the Sigman explained that the device was incapable of emitting substances harmful to humans. With practice, they grew able to imitate a growing variety of known foods. Yvonne found relaxation in developing comestibles Earth had never seen.

The Sigman fed itself from a similar device in the same room. "This virtually proves what has been suspected," Wang declared. "They have made previous expeditions here, which carried out intensive biological studies. The ship arrived ready to house men."

A third silveriness gave clean water. "Now if only I could figure how to make ethyl alcohol without live yeast," Skip murmured. But he didn't really miss drugs, not in this delirium of revelation.

Body wastes and organic trash were dropped at random on the resilient decks. Within seconds they were recognized and absorbed, returned to the closed ecology of the ship. (Or the life of the ship? More and more it seemed as if the vessel was not akin to a robot but to a plant-animal symbiosis, drawing energy from its private thermonuclear sun, nourishment from the gas and stones of space.)

The environment required adaptation. Air was always thick, hot, and humid by terrestrial cahons, though well within mammalian tolerance. Skip borrowed a pair of scissors, reduced his trousers to shorts, and wore nothing else. His companions stayed with their regular garb.

The intense orange-yellow light caused headaches until the Sigman demonstrated how to make local adjustments and have any illumination desired. Odors were everywhere, rich and strange. A terrestrial greenhouse was bleak by comparison. Some took a little getting used to, but most were enjoyable from the start—suggestive of green growth, spices, roses, ocean beaches, thunderstorms, a woman's sunlit hair, uncountably much, whole worlds full of life and weather. In like wise, tones pervaded the interior, resonant, sibilant, everything man could hear and probably a great deal man could not, single notes or melodies. (Melodies? The patterns, though equally pleasing, were too complex to identify as music. But then, a savage who has known only voice and drum might find the *Tod und Verklärung* bewildering.)

Nothing was monotonous. These many stimuli, and no doubt more which did not reach skin-enclosed human nerves, kept changing. Breezes followed calm, dimness followed brightness, temperature and humidity and ionization were not constant, fresh aromas and sounds replaced those of a minute ago, sometimes the deck would ripple underfoot—you never felt imprisoned aboard the Sigman argosy.

Its geometry alone guaranteed that. Beyond the barrier dome, which now stood permanently open, lay no rigid structure of halls and cabins. Corridors wound in labyrinthine loops. The Earthlings, who were free to roam them, would soon have been lost had the alien not pointed out how the plants which grew in some, the glowing cryptic murals which decorated others, doubled as a system of indicators. ("For our benefit," Yvonne guessed. "Our friend doesn't need signposts.") Evidently a passageway could bulge inward on command, forming a room of adjustable size and shape, almost anyplace. The Sigman obliged its guests with separate chambers and sealable entrances. Rubbery daises grew from their decks. Skip amused himself at the control area of his apartment, adding an easy chair and, at the point where water flowed in response to a gesture, washbasin and bathtub.

All this was done and learned in the course of the first few earth-days. It was mere preliminary to what came after.

There was an observation turret, but that is the wrong word. The humans stood on a transparent bridge, at the center of a great hollow sphere which reproduced the view outside. Reproduction was not absolutely faithful; the dangerous brightness of the sun was stepped down and actinic radiation must be omitted; but otherwise the simulacrum was more truly *space* than what men had ever before seen through window or helmet. The Sigman was elsewhere, tending the conn it had not yet shown them. They were braking down toward Mars.

In silence and night, they almost forgot how steamy the air was. Stars in their myriads glittered winter-keen, the Milky Way cataracted around heaven, the far small sun burned within a pearly lens of zodiacal light. Ahead loomed the planet, gibbous between white northern polar cap and antarctic duskiness, a hundred different umbers and rust-reds dappled blue-gray-green and one tawny dust storm, crater scars waxing naked-eye visible, a vision whose austerity transcended itself and became purity. Yet the glow therefrom which fell upon the humans and evoked their faces from the dark was hearthfire-soft.

Wang broke a long hush. He spoke low, with none of the stiffness he had used before: "My younger son dreams of being a cosmonaut. He said to me once, if we get ships like this he will renounce the ambition, for the work should not be easy. I approved of his attitude. Now I wonder whether he may have been mistaken."

"I think he was," Yvonne replied. "Is Beethoven easy, or El Greco, or Aeschylus?"

"My little girl would love this sight," Wang said. A smile touched him. "She might ask why no bough of peach blossoms crosses the funny moon."

Abruptly, as if shying, his tone grew parched and he continued: "Why were we taken here? Men have been on Mars, and the Sigman has made repeated visits. What is its motive?"

"Several, I'd guess," Skip answered. "First, practicality. At long last people have shown they can present something that makes the trouble of building a common language worthwhile. For that, it's handier having weight. Second, if we're going to accelerate, why not a Cook's tour? In fact, that gives endless opportunities to compare notes and—well, like the captain and I do pictures of the same planetscape, acquire techniques we'd never have thought of—isn't this what it wants from us? Our science and engineering are ridiculous. Our biology and so forth were described maybe thousands of years ago. But a cross-fertilization of arts—"

"As China influenced Europe in the eighteenth century," Wang nodded, "or Africa did later."

"Or Buddhist motifs from India affected China earlier," Skip said, "and they in their turn had been affected by the Greeks. Or take the Eighteenth Dynasty of Egypt, most brilliant period they ever had, because for a short while they allowed in a breath from Crete and Syria. Well, you get the idea. The third motive for this trip—" He stopped.

"What is that?"

"Never mind."

Wang's eyes, which had been filled with Mars-light, swung to him. The others could see how he tautened. "Are you scheming behind my back again?"

"Oh, dry up," Skip said in anger, "and blow away." He struck the rail with a fist. "Do you have to trot out your grievances every hour on the hour? Okay, chum, I'll tell you what I think the third reason is for leaving Earth's neighborhood. To prevent any more dismal nuisances like you from joining the party."

"Skip." Yvonne caught his arm. "Please."

"Best I withdraw. My regrets, Dr. Canter." Wang bowed and walked on down the bridge. He was soon lost among the star clouds.

The ship carried tenders for visiting planetary surfaces. In one of these, the four beings descended to Mars, skimmed across thousands of kilometers, hovered near the ground for closer looks. Their craft was a lean, tapered cylindroid; save for enclosures that must contain engine, controls, and instruments, its hull was practically invisible. "To radar also, I presume," Wang said. His voice trailed off. The same thought stirred in the three human minds: *What a bomber, what a missile!*

Yvonne said in haste, to repair the fragile truce, "But harmful rays have to be blocked. Sigma Draconis is cooler than Sol, gives off less ultraviolet. That should mean the life there is more vulnerable to UV and the rest than we are."

"Me, I'd give a pretty to know what drives this critter," Skip said. No jets or rockets or propellers did, nothing discernible, nor was anything to be heard save the ghost-thin screech of cloven Martian air as the desert reeled away beneath. "Hydromagnetics? Insufficient in open space, maybe, but when a large mass is nearby to react against—" He walked forward to the Sigman, a pair of whose lobster-octopus hands were making pilot's motions. The rear eyestalks extended toward him. He opened his sketchbook.

"What do you plan?" Wang asked suspiciously.

"Why, find out if our buddy has investigated Earth. A boat like this could travel unnoticed, except maybe in a rare glimpse that the glimpser 'ud take for a mirage or a speck in his aqueous humor or maybe he should swear off the sauce. Anyhow, it could if it avoided densely populated areas, or observed 'em from high altitudes. And you wouldn't really want to park in Times Square, would you?"

Skip ascertained that his idea was right. He suspected the Sigman had avoided making contact on those flights lest it be detained in a gravity it could not long endure. He suspected further that remote sightings of architectural masterpieces were all that had encouraged it to keep trying with genus Homo.

Shortly afterward, they made their first of several landings. Spacesuited, they went outside. The Sigman's protec-

tion resembled a clear plastic sack drawn snug around
limbs and lower body, loose on top to leave the sensor
tendrils unhampered. ("Why does pressure not stiffen it
like a balloon?" Wang wondered, and found no answer.)
The sites must have been chosen forethoughtfully, because
they did not sustain the generally drab impression which
terrestrial explorers had brought home. A dunescape
rolled in muted red and black; a cliff stood vivid with
ores; a crag reared stark against dark-purple heaven. Be-
like the Sigman was disappointed to learn how badly Skip
was hampered by his gloves, and cut the tour short in
order that drawing and painting might continue.

Mars dwindled aft. The ship drove on outward.

Somehow the humans took to calling the Sigman
Ahasuerus. They failed to establish whether its race had
nomenclature. "I would guess not, in our sense," Yvonne
said. "Not a noise attached to an individual. Instead, a
whole complex of associations, appearance, personality,
scent, stance, the entire identity remembered and reproduced in a cluster of symbolic acts when identification is
required." Musingly: "*If* it is. Sigman individuality may
have fundamental differences from the human kind. The
clues we've gotten thus far—"

Nonetheless Ahasuerus the Wanderer quickly learned to
utter a special sound that meant a particular guest. And it
took the initiative in developing certain imperatives. Between Mars and Jupiter it frequently said, "Yvonne Canter and Wang Li, go. Skip stay." Or: "Skip come with me.
Yvonne Canter and Wang Li, do not bother us if you
come too."

Those were the occasions when it wanted to pursue
study of the terrestrial material, or show off work of its
own—which was not readily describable in human language—or compare methods of depicting a particular subject, like a flower or a part of the heavens. Wang soon
used up its interest in his calligraphy, and thereafter the
linguists were often ignored.

They put those episodes to use, planning further vocabulary and grammar against Ahasuerus' next session with
the vocal synthesizer. Gradually their mutual wariness
diminished. "I understand that you cannot be blamed for
policies forced upon you by your government," Wang said
once when they two were alone. "Indeed, you are to be
pitied. Your life twice endangered—"

"Twice!" she exclaimed, startled. "How did you know that?"

Wang showed a moment's chagrin. "I spoke rashly. You are right, the news was not released." He took the offensive. "Why not?"

"To avoid making a bad situation worse." She backed a step from him. "You have spies among us, then."

"And you among us," he retorted. Turning mild: "Yes, I was informed of your second misadventure. I do regret the trouble, I do wish you will have no more. For your sake I beg you, put away your naïveté."

"What do you mean, Professor Wang?"

"You are too trusting. You actually believe that the news about you was suppressed for altruistic reasons. Have you never thought that its broadcasting might entail the release of other facts the American government would prefer to keep secret?" Wang's voice was metallic: "Is the young man who accompanies you really the simple-minded boor he pretends? What influence is he exerting on the Sigman at this moment? What has he discovered, what has he conveyed, that you and I have not been told of?"

Heat and cold washed through Yvonne. Her foot thudded against the deck. "Stop that!" she cried. Later her vehemence would astonish her. "Skip's the most honest, bravest— All right, he doesn't have a proper Chinese reverence for age and position, but we have him alone to thank we're here today and, and, and when I was kidnapped he went into the Underworld and found a man who knew where I might be and talked him into—" Sobs overran her. "If you knew how sick I am of people accusing people! What race of Satan Mekatrigs are we, a-a-anyway?" She whirled and fled.

At their next meeting, they traded formal apologies. The breach was healed anew. *But every time,* she thought— and concurrently thought that this was a Skip way of putting it—*the scab is thinner.*

Jupiter, imperial world, vast amber shield richly banded in clouds that are ocher and bronze, dimmed greens and blues, twilight violet, furnace jewel of the Red Spot where four Earths could lie side by side, ruling a moonswarm whose chieftains could be small planets: your grandeur is only less terrible than the sun's.

Skip floated in the observation globe, tethered to the bridge, and let his gaze drown in the sight around which he orbited. Its radiance drenched him and Yvonne, at this distance surpassing fifty full Lunas upon Earth, over-whelming the stars and flooding the watchers in gold. They were alone.

She said finally, "I cannot understand why Ahasuerus isn't here also, looking."

His mind was slow to come back to her. What drew him at last was the light, molten in tears that broke from her fluttering lashes and drifted off into the silence. He thought of Danaë, and wished he could find a better answer than: "Reckon it's gone to bed, like Wang. No-body's tireless. Wang's not young, and Ahasuerus has had a rough day. Two and a half gravities, when you're evolved for oh-point-three—imagine."

"You?" Her fingers strayed to his shoulder.

"M-m, I'm pretty fagged and battered myself. Astrono-mers kept telling me and telling me, Jupiter's uppermost atmosphere has storms in it that'd blow out a terrestrial hurricane, they told me. But no, I had to go fly a boat there." Skip's levity faded. His eyes returned to the Shin-ing One. "Worth it," he whispered, "a million times over. The vapor banks, taller than mountains, wider than vision can reach, rising, tumbling, lightning alive in them and the colors, the colors. . . ."

"You were crazily reckless to go, Skip. Please don't again."

"I will if Ahasuerus will." He turned about and caught her hand. "Look, Yvonne, the jaunt today was its idea. I figured it knew what a tender can and cannot do. And when it showed me how to pilot the boat, let me take over in the Jovian air—Lord, surfing isn't in the same class!" He paused. "No worries. That funny harness supported us perfectly well, and tyro though I was, I never lost control. You know, I suspect that's what Ahasuerus has in mind. It's worse handicapped in high gravity than we are. Man-Sigman partnership—what can't we do!"

She sighed. He cocked his head. "You look unhappy," he murmured. "Problems?"

"N-n-nothing." She averted her glance. "Tired. Emo-tional strain. . . . No, don't blame Wang Li. I'm simply that kind of person." She wiped her face. "And to tell the truth, this tropical climate is grinding me down. Do you think we could arrange for a room to be kept cool and dry?"

"Probably, if we can get the message across. However, you could be comfortable right now if you'd shuck that mess you're wearing." Skip's gesture went from her cover-

all to his shorts. "Let Wang be a good self-abnegating
Communist and maintain the dignity of the Party in his
brown outfit. You and I don't need more than pockets.
Why, at weights from zero to one-third, you can omit a
brassiere and not sag. Which I don't imagine you do
anyway."

The Jupiter-light was so brilliant that he saw her flush.
He cupped her chin in his left hand, laid his right on her
hip, and said, "Yvonne, your Ortho itself dropped nudity
taboos outside of completely public places before I was
born. We've both seen square kilometers of assorted human skin, and this is hardly a public place. Nobody's
about to force his attentions on you. Why are you scared
to be comfortable?"

She breathed in and out and in again, teeth clamped
together, until: "All right!" she ripped out, half in
defiance, and pulled the garment off before she could lose
courage.

"Marvelous," Skip laughed. "I did not promise not to
admire. You're beautiful."

"I'd better go," she said shakily. "Goodnight." She released the tether to her belt, held the coverall across her
front, and pulled herself along by the rail. Skip stayed,
watching her move through the rain of gold.

Ahasuerus indicated Saturn was next. That would be a
long reach, especially when the sixth planet was nowhere
near conjunction with Jupiter.

The four aboard settled down to a systematic quest for
comprehension. This did not mean that the Sigman now
spent most of its time in the presence of the sound
synthesizer. In fact, spoken language remained the least
part of its effort. Twice as much went to Skip and the
graphic and sculptural arts, thrice as much to whatever
it did when humans were not around. (Likeliest it worked
on its own projects, Skip thought, or simply contem-
plated the movement of a leaf, the blueness of a star.)

But Ahasuerus did show more patience with the
linguists than hitherto. Either it had decided that in the
end it would have to communicate with Earthlings via
speech; or Skip had gotten that idea across by the half-
intuitive hieroglyphics which were developing between him
and the Sigman; or something else had happened inside
that nonhuman awareness. Whatever the reason, the synthesizer now averaged two or three hours per day in use.

Progress was helped by the circumstance that, increasingly, Ahasuerus could read Skip's terrestrial-style drawings and he could read its fiery networks in the air. And each was mastering the other's pictorial technique.

Yvonne soon forgot the skimpiness of her present garb. Wang forgot his disapproval of it. They were both too busy, holding verbal sessions, analyzing the results, planning for the future. "We are two attempting the task of a score," he said ruefully. "We are fortunate that, between us, we command a variety of languages. But I wish we had speakers of Arunta, Nahua, Dravidian, Xosa—"

"—the whole race of man," she finished, and brushed a damp black lock of hair off her brow. "Well, when we return, maybe. . . . I pray to the God I don't believe in, let this bring us Earthfolk together."

He made no reply. The unspoken thought hung between them: *Thus far it has driven us more apart.*

Work took them in its arms and gave them discovery. They had reached the threshold of being able to ask questions.

Answers emerged, swiftly or slowly depending on obviousness. The ship was in truth from Sigma Draconis, the second planet of the star. The planet had about a fourth of Earth's diameter, and a lower mean density. That was no surprise; and comparing the size and atmosphere of Venus, you began to wonder if Earth might not be a freak, holding less air than a world its size and temperature was entitled to. (Ask, ask! The Sigmans have visited scores of suns, these past x thousand years.) There were seas and land masses, the latter in islands rather than true continents. There was no natural satellite. The rotation period was approximately 50 hours, the axial inclination scant, the year about a fourth again the length of Earth's . . . no, wait, can't be right, the planet would be farther out and therefore cooler . . . no, the star's less massive . . . let the astronomers decide. A whole new cosmology will open for them.

Sister globes— Not yet. First let us inquire into the sentience born of that one world. What use the universe without life that can wonder at it?

Several of the strictly biological puzzles were cleared away in short order. The guess turned out to be correct, that Sigman bodies lacked the multifarious interior specializations of human. What separate organs identifiably existed were primitive by comparison with a stomach, a gonad, a brain. The tendency always was for a given kind of cell—far larger, more elaborate and versatile than any terrestrial analog—to handle a variety of functions. In like manner, the species had a single sex, though two partners were needed for impregnation: of both, who both gave live birth. Apparently matings were for life, and apparently life was for centuries.

Subtler questions could, at the present stage, only have inferential answers which might well prove wrong. But slowly the tentative conclusions grew:

Sigmans did live and think at a more leisured rate than men. The same was not true of perception; they swam in an ocean of sense data and responded to nuances on almost the molecular level. Pheromones played an enormous role between persons, as did the most delicate cues of every other kind. While speech was well developed and writing highly so, these were mere parts of language— useful, for certain purposes essential, yet never to be mistaken for the whole.

And that whole was in turn a unitary part of the world. Doubtless individual Sigmans varied as much as individual humans do. Nonetheless Yvonne's conjecture looked right, that individuality itself was more diffuse, less clearly demarcated from the rest of reality, than ever on Earth. ("Super-Zen," Skip said.) This helped explain how Ahasuerus could spend years on end alone. It did not, by its own standards, have an eremitical personality. It did have indefinitely many subpersonalities to interact; and none of these felt isolated when they perceived an entire cosmos around them. Eventually the traveler would long back home. But it was in no hurry. Here it had magnificence to explore and depict and become one with.

Esthetics might well have been the prime evolutionary factor calling forth intelligence on the Sigman planet. Theories held that curiosity had done this for man's ancestors. The trait was of survival value in making an animal learn the dangers and possibilities of the environment. Conceivably the ancestral pre-Sigman, being already open to its surroundings and intensely aware of them, benefited correspondingly from a drive first to seek, later to create harmonious conditions of life. Thus when the scientific method appeared, it was less a technique for expanding the realm of precise knowledge than for reducing intellectual chaos to a set of elegant solutions.

Of course, man had the latter ideal too, and doubtless the Sigmans had curiosity. The difference was in emphasis. In either species, technology soon took pragmatic advantage of scientific findings. If Yvonne's and Wang's impression was right, war had always been unknown among the Sigmans and destruction of land or befouling of waters, which ran counter to instinct, were rare. Thus the machine was mostly a benefactor.

This did not mean Sigmans were natural saints. They might be less capable than man of devotion to a group or an ideal, more prone to callous exploitation of their fellow individuals. That was sheer speculation. However, Ahasuerus' failure to grasp certain ideas like infinity was almost unambiguously shown. (Draw a series of larger and larger triangles on the same base. The two rising sides will become more and more nearly parallel. Draw them, at last, exactly parallel, breaking your pencil lines somewhere and pointing to indicate that the ideal lines continue. Ahasuerus never took that final step; instead, it made noises of negation. You could nearly hear it thinking: "But they *don't.*") Maybe humankind had something to teach Sigmankind in mathematics as well as art. . . in philosophy, in poetry and music and dance. . . . There are many more kinds of love than the sexual. What kinds might arise between the comrades of two races, three, four, a thousand, a million?

"Oh, glory, glory," Skip chanted to the stars, until the hour came when everything was ruined.

XIV

———◆———

Far under the spaceboat the clouds of Saturn lay like a continent, plains, mountains, canyons, slow smoky rivers. They were white and dim gold, the shadows upon them were royal blue, and off the brightest was reflected a ghost of the rings above. Yvonne kept her gaze mainly on the rings themselves. Against blackness and stars they soared, gigantic rainbows sparked with moving, twinkling points of prismatic light, overwhelmingly awesome, impossibly lovely.

"I am reluctant," Wang said into the silence. "But we had better return."

She nodded. He glanced at the instrumental displays which hovered above the control cubicle and moved his fingers beneath them. Acceleration pushed bodies back into seats, and the continent dwindled toward a spheroid.

Wang activated the broadcast transmitter. "Hello, ship," he said. "We are bound back. How shall we rendezvous?"

A monitor was set to notify Skip, and radio outlets were everywhere in the mother vessel. His voice came in a minute: "Hi. Did you have a good time?"

" 'Good' is a poor little word," Yvonne answered mutedly.

"Yeah. How well I know," Skip said. "Not that I'm sorry I stayed aboard. Tell you 'bout it when you arrive. . . . Lemme check, uh, with Ahasuerus. . . . Simplest is if you make for Titan. At one gee. We'll intercept. Can do?"

"Yes." Wang repeated the plan and signed off. His hands called for a projection of the local system. In its alien style it resembled a schematic drawing. He identified the largest moon and indicated that he wished to go there at the specified acceleration. The boat turned its nose through an arc and lined out.

When he learned that Skip had been taught to operate

137

the tenders—as he did on the first trip into this atmosphere—Wang had insisted on the same privilege. There
wasn't much to convey. A computer (?) did nearly everything. Crossing space in such a vehicle was safer and
easier than piloting a car manually on an empty highway.

Then Ahasuerus made known that it wished to shuttle
around the planet, presumably to view at various angles
and distances, for some hours before starting sunward.
Yvonne and Wang wanted to repeat the near-religious
experience of seeing the rings from below. They had
already observed them afar, and superb though that had
been, it was not the same. Skip thought likewise, but the
Sigman was insistent he remain. It raised no objection to
the proposal that his companions revisit the primary. Saturn was perfectly safe, at any rate if you stayed in the
upper stratosphere. Receiving less than a third of the
slight solar energy that Jupiter gets, those layers are calm,
and at their height the force of gravity is scarcely more
than on Earth.

Yvonne stirred. "If we could tell them when we get
home," she said. "Tell them in a way to make them
believe. How little we are, we humans; how big we could
be; how squalid our intrigues and quarrels."

"I think they already know," Wang replied, "apart from
a few monsters. Unhappily, a number of the monsters are
at the levers of power, which requires honest men to
respond in kind."

Yvonne felt a sad smile cross her. "Nobody can agree
which is which." She spoke no further. Her wistfulness
could not last, beneath that bridge to the gods.

They stood in the observation chamber and watched the
world recede. Wang and Ahasuerus occupied one end of
the bridge. He was making a poem about it, and the
Sigman was keeping an eye of its four on the characters
he drew. Yvonne moved to the opposite end in order that
she not distract or be distracted.

Still the planet was vast and radiant. The light was less
than from Jupiter, more argent than aureate, though also
equaling many terrestrial moons. The cloud bands were
not spectacularly colored or turbulent. But the rings! And
ahead, near the tiny sun, arched an immense white bow,
Titan; she had stood on its eternal snows, looked through
the dusk-blue of its thin air at Saturn hanging above a
mountain range, and cried.

A hand fell over hers where it lay on the rail. She felt

the smoothness and warmth of skin that brushed her arm, and through the myriad Sigman scents drifted an odor of humanness. "Mind if I join you?" Skip asked quietly. "I won't burble the way I did when you came aboard."

Her heart knocked. "Please do stay. You never told me what happened while I was gone."

He hesitated. "Well . . . we had an interesting time. We'd orbit first here, next there, and do renderings and— Let's not talk shop. This place has really put you on trajectory, hasn't it?"

"Hasn't it you?"

"What else?"

She turned to face him. In the faerie light he stood as if cast in silver and crowned with stars. "And we can come back," she jubilated. "Ahasuerus wants us in the universe. Doesn't it?"

Again he took a moment to answer. "Yes. Very much." When he moved, shadows flowed among the muscles of arm and belly.

"We can come back," she repeated. "We can go on. Every dream our race has ever dreamed— It's like, for me it's like when I was newly married— No. That was always alloyed with dailiness. This . . . Do you remember the turn of the century?"

"Sure. My gang, neighborhood boys, we got hold of some highly illegal fireworks and shot them off. Police and parents didn't do more than scold us. It was that kind of night."

"You were pre-adolescent, though. I was in my late teens. An age when the awkwardness is outlived, the hopefulness newborn, everything a miracle. And there the new century—the new millennium!—stood before us. A portal, where we'd leave all that was bad, worn-out, sordid, and run through the gate unburdened, clean, free. Into a land nobody had spoiled, the promised land. This is the same. Only it's not a youthful illusion now, it's real. It's forever!"

She embraced him. "And Skip, you won it for us. You, none but you."

He was holding her. She pulled back. He did not let go. She raised her cheek from his breast and found his mouth waiting. After a minute that whirled, she broke free and cast an apprehensive glance past him, down the invisible bridge. Silhouetted athwart the Milky Way, as if hovering free among clustered stars, Ahasuerus' pinecone bulk still screened her from Wang. Skip took her by the hair and gently, irresistibly recalled her to him. His hand traveled on down her back. His other hand— Hers were over his neck, his shoulders, his ribs. "No . . . please . . . o-o-oh. . . . Why not? Why have I been this slow?

"Come on, darling, darling. Saturn can wait. We'll be back. My cabin—" Between laughter and tears: "I came prepared. I didn't think to, but when I unpacked my personal kit I found— Rings are for lovers."

The Sigman intended to stop at innermost Mercury. Orbit to orbit, that would require about fifteen days. From there, swinging still nearer the sun, it would return to Earth. (Evidently it found Venus as unattractive at close quarters as men did.) "And we'll be let off," Skip said.

Yvonne snuggled into the curve of his arm. "I won't know whether to be glad or sad," she told him. "Both, I suppose." Her fingers at the base of his spine said, *Always glad while we are together.*

Wang ignored her. He had made no comment on what had clearly been happening between them. An average Westerner would have offered congratulations. *I suppose the poor prim dear thinks we're awful,* Yvonne reflected, and pressed closer against Skip.

"Will we be allowed to take a ship's boat?" Wang asked.

They were seated on temporarily extruded couches in what had been the original reception area for humans. The scientific apparatus remained there, making it a natural meeting place. (*And we really should instigate regular dining here. Skip and I share our meals, from the planning and making to the last bite and a kiss for dessert. Wang eats all alone.*) Ahasuerus was not present. The open dome, the rustling fragrant garden beyond, reminded of the being who, Skip said he had learned, came eighteen light-years to renew on behalf of its people the sense of marvel their distant ancestors had brought back from Sol.

Wang had replied: "Do you not think the time is overpast for you to share with us—with me—the knowledge you have gained in your special sessions? This project was supposed to exemplify the ideal of international cooperation." And thus the conference had been arranged.

Skip creased his brows. "Well?" Wang urged.

"Okay, I'll speak frankly," Skip said. "I'm not certain. Ahasuerus and I haven't got a secret code that we sent away our box tops for, as you imagine."

Wang stiffened yet more, and Yvonne thought, *I must*

persuade my darling to act respectful. He doesn't mean harm—usually—but Wang can't understand banter, takes it for insult and replies in kind, and then Skip gets angry, and the feedback goes on and on till now they raise hackles at sight of each other.

Maybe the sigaroon noticed, for he continued in an ordinary tone: "Not knowing the use of the sound synthesizer, I can't do Sigman imitations. We swap some words, but mainly we draw pictures. We've arrived at a lot of conventional signs, yes, and I'll make a dictionary of them if you wish. I will for sure in my official report. On the whole, though, we depend on intuition for understanding. It's like trying to read a comic strip where most of the words didn't get printed."

"You have explained that before," Wang said, not quite implying disbelief. "I asked what your impression, if you will—what your impression is of our being given or lent a tender for our descent to Earth."

"My impression is we could have one if we asked. Or if I asked. Let's talk plain: Yvonne first learned how to speak with Ahasuerus, but I'm its lodge brother." Skip fondled her. "That it prefers my company to hers proves how alien it is." He dropped back to seriousness. "I don't think we should ask. I won't make the request. Our astronauts can take us off same as before."

Wang kept motionless. Yvonne looked into Skip's face, which had stopped being boyish, and inquired, troubled, "Why?"

"You know why," he answered. "Too tempting for governments. I believe the catchword is 'destabilization.' "

"You may be right, Mr. Wayburn," Wang said slowly.

Skip raised himself on an elbow. The forearm was under her neck, the hand on her farther side. His free hand and a foot moved along her, lingering. The light in the cabin was set low and rosy. "You're an angel," he whispered.

She reached up to stroke him in return. "I'm happy enough to be," she said, no louder. "A fallen angel, though."

His lips quirked. "Fallen, or tumbled?"

"Both. *Damn* well tumbled."

"Fallen souls together, then. Free falling ... hey, how 'bout that sometime? . . . falling free forever and ever."

He lowered himself to nuzzle the hollow where throat met shoulder. And the delicious leisurely rearousing from drowsiness went from her, swift as a knife stab. She gripped him and said in her terror, "Do you mean that? Do you?"

"Yes," he said into her hair. "Here beside you, I finally mean it for good."

"So you've felt the same about others?"

He caught the raw note, released her, and sat up. His eyes rested grave upon her. "I catch. Yes, once in a while before, I've just as honestly supposed it was for always. Only you're different, Vonny. Nobody's like you."

She joined him, resting her back against the headboard they had shaped onto the dais when they doubled its width. She clung to his hand with her entire strength, but stared straight forward. Her voice ran quick and uneven:

"Oh, yes, I have education, position— No, please don't misunderstand, I realize you want absolutely nothing from me except myself. We work and talk well together. Probably I'm the brightest woman you've met. You're bright too, you like to learn and think. I teach you things and challenge your mind." Her head drooped. "What else? I'm not the best-looking. Don't flatter me. I'm striking. Maybe I first began to fall in love when you showed me how striking I am, ages ago on that ocean ship. But I'm no beauty queen. I'm barely on the good side of skinny. I'm trying to learn how to please you, but you must have had pupils more apt. And . . . when I'm forty, you'll be thirty-two. When you're forty-two, I'll be fifty."

"Won't matter," he said.

"Because you'll be long gone? That often keeps me awake after you've fallen asleep. I lie there listening to you breathe and I think, 'Under the best circumstances we're bound to have a hard go of it. But he's an eagle and I'm a dove.' "

"Now you romanticize," he drawled. "Why not call me a goose and you chicken?"

She fought the tears and lost. He held her. "I'm sorry," he told her again and again. "I shouldn't've joked. It's my way, not my wish. I'd not hurt you for . . . for this whole flinkin' starcraft."

When at length she rested more calmly, he gave her a quizzical regard. "Wrong time of month coming on?" he asked.

She gulped and nodded. "Feels like it."

"Doesn't make what you said less important, no. But might make it more miserable than needful."

"Uh-huh." She attempted a smile. "Curses, how I wish we had cigarettes along! Next trip we'll know."

"Atta girl." He stroked her cheek a while. Then, seating himself on the edge of the bed so he could look into her eyes while he held her hands, he said:

"Vonny, if I were in the habit of fretting about the future like you, I'd for sure be afraid. Seems to me you're likelier to get tired and kick me out than I am to drift off. But we'll just have to try it and see. I do want to try, try my utmost to make this thing last. You *are* wonderful." He drew breath. "To prove it, I'll tell you something I hadn't made up my mind to tell anybody. Maybe I shouldn't, I dunno, but I want to give you everything I have."

For an instant she was reminded of her youngest brother, who when he was five and she was having her fourteenth birthday had come shyly, adoringly to press on her a smudged and skewed model rocket glider he had assembled himself.

"I know how this vessel works," Skip said.

She straightened.

He nodded. "Yeah. When Ahasuerus and I were batting around Saturn. It wanted me to conn while it took a boat outside a while. I think it's sensitive to the Doppler shift and wanted to incorporate it in a painting, but I couldn't swear to that. Anyway, it gave me the lesson. Easy. The single real trick is getting into the control room. You have to semaphore exactly right or the wall won't open. There's another special set of signals to activate the engines. Fail-safe precaution. I imagine. Otherwise it's hardly different from operating a tender. You stand in a miniature version of the viewroom and use a scaled-up version of the navigator displays. Then you can leave her on automatic till you get where you're bound. Shucks, I could take us interstellar. The material's on file for this entire galactic neighborhood. Just start the Bussard intake when you're up to ram scoop speed and kick in the photon drive when you're sure it won't harm anything local."

"Ahasuerus must really trust us," she breathed.

His mouth stretched his face into lumps and gullies. "That's the trouble," he said. "It takes for granted we're as . . . innocent . . . as the few other atomic-era species it knows of. Could the rest have wiped themselves out?"

"I see why you're keeping silence."

"Uh-huh. I was bubbling over at first, you may recall. Mainly I figured I'd better not let on to Wang. Since, I've been thinking, and the more I think the more doubtful I am. He himself agrees it'd be unwise to give our military types a tender, even though they prob'ly couldn't duplicate it any more than Marconi could've duplicated a transistorized TV set. But the ship! You don't need to build a fleet. This one is plenty. You send a delegation here—and Ahasuerus is going to welcome delegations from now on, if they bring artwork—and the delegation takes Ahasuerus prisoner or kills it, and there they are, the owners of humanity."

She thought, *He loves me enough to share his fears.* She said, "Can't you convince the Sigman it must never tell anyone else?"

"I've been trying. Not easy to make clear a message like that."

"And you— Thank mercy you're the one, Skip!" She reached for him. He remained where he was and said:

"If you mean we're lucky because I'll keep the whole matter secret, don't make book, Vonny. Should I?"

"What? Of course—"

"Is it that 'of course'? Suppose the power did fall to America. I'm no flagflapper, but I don't despise my country either. Seems to me, by and large America's more decent than most, and has the size and strength to maintain peace. I'm not convinced those rickety international arrangements we've got will last much longer. Look how they're starting to come apart already. Pax Americana—is a lousy solution like that better'n no solution? Or would it work at all?" He shook his head. "I don't know. Do you?"

"No," she said. "But I have faith—"

"Is faith good enough? Think, please, Vonny. Use that well-oiled brain of yours." Impudence could not help flickering forth in a grin. "Along with a well-oiled body, hm-m-m?" Bleak again: "I want your advice. However, in the end, you realize, I'll have to decide. Me, alone with myself."

Mercury was crags and craters under a black sky, by day a giant sun whose light ran like wildfire, here and there pools of molten metal that congealed by night and sheened with starshine—tormented grandeur.

Yvonne thought she understood how the boat's hull protected her from glare and maybe from short-wave radiation. Its transparency was self-darkening in proportion to need. She did not know how she stayed no warmer than usual, when the outside temperature neared 700 degrees Kelvin. Well, if they meant to skirt Sol— Could the right interplay of electric and magnetic fields control, not only charged particles but neutral ones and quanta? She wasn't sure if that was theoretically possible. She was, though, sure that the theories of Earthside physicists were not the last word.

Her speculation was a vague rippling across the unhappiness which filled most of her.

At the rear of the boat, Skip and Ahasuerus excitedly collaborated on a rendition in oils and Sigman pigments of a glitterstorm. Blown on the wisp of air that remained to this world, the fine micalike particles brought out the brutal mass of a cliff behind them.

How can he be merry when fate has touched him?—I grow hourly more aware of the guilt which is ours, no matter what course we choose. And that awareness makes me less and less his kind of woman, and he feels rebuffed, and I don't pretend very well, and so he may leave me as soon as his foot touches Earth, and might that be for the best? And I pray, how I pray he won't.

Beside her in the bows, Wang lowered the movie camera he had borrowed from their regular scientific equipment. "I must have private copies of this sequence, if of nothing else I have taken," he said. "My daughter loves fireflies."

The other day, for the first time, he showed me her picture. "I'd like to meet your daughter," Yvonne said.

"Do." He sounded as if he meant it. "We will be honored to receive you in our home."

Will you? After my country has seared a city or two of yours into slag, to prove it can melt and burn everything that four thousand years of China has given us, if you don't let in its occupation troops?

"And I am hopeful that in due course we can return the visit," Wang was saying. "Already she has heard about Disneyland." He sighed. "I went there once and found it frivolous. But that is what our past two or three generations have labored for since the Revolution, that P'ing's shall have time for the fullness of culture, self-development, and, yes, a little frivolity."

If you're still living on promises after two or three generations, won't she too? You can't simply bring her to see me, because if you go abroad your family has to stay hostage behind. Dare I tell Skip such a government ought not to be obliterated for the safety, the very survival of mankind?—But dare I say it cannot evolve, that it has not already evolved, that it will never give us a better gift than Caesar's ignoble peace?

Would such a peace even last? Rome tore itself apart. Byzantium decayed.

Have I no faith in my countrymen? What if we tell Andy Almeida that we, Skip, can run the starship? Will Andy have irons clapped on Skip, and drug and torture him till he shows how? Will Andy's superiors? I voted for President Braverman. He sits in the house of Thomas Jefferson. —But Hitler started in gemütlich old Bavaria, didn't he? —What to do, what to do?

The surface pull of Mercury gave slightly less weight than the normal acceleration of the ship. Yet it was as if already Yvonne could feel Earth's heaviness upon her.

You had read the figures: Photosphere diameter 1,390,-000 kilometers, mass 329,390 times the terrestrial, energy output converting 560,000,000 tons per second of matter into radiation, prominences rising to more than 150,000 kilometers, corona extending several times as far, solar wind blowing to the remotest planetary orbit and beyond. You had seen photographs, astronomical cinema, transmissions from unmanned probes. It was interesting. It was gossip about your old friend Sol, that altogether ordinary yellow dwarf star which was expected to keep reliably lighting the world for another five billion years. You had to watch yourself with Sol, of course. He was boisterous. He could garble your favorite television program or give you a red and peeling nose. When he got really rough, if you weren't careful he might strike you dead. But at heart he was a good fellow, steady old Sol.

Then you found that none of this had anything to do with that which, no matter how stepped down and baffled and buffered, flamed before you.

Sunward of Mercury, you saw at first an unutterable white splendor, swirled with storms, maned with a huge lacy rain that fountained outward and intricately down again, surrounded by an effulgence that shimmered pearl and mother-of-pearl among the stars—there are no words. But you ran nearer, and it grew, it ate the sky, its burning, burning, burning became everything that was, fire roared around, somehow a part of the fury came through and the ship rang to it, bellow and shriek and whistle and high sweet singing; a gout of red and yellow and green and hell-blue that could cremate your planet came brawling toward you, you couldn't help yourself but had to shut your eyes and cover your ears, and the torrent raged past, engulfing you, its rumble in your marrow to fill you with fear—

And through those hours he would not hold you, he shouted you should hide in your cabin if you didn't like the show, well, he had been angry with you and you had to prove you weren't a coward so you stayed, but he and his friend didn't want you near, they were ripping forth lines, splashing gobs of color on surfaces, they were wild as the Ragnarok around them—

But the stiff gray man who loved his small daughter, he stood by, he let you cling to him and gave you the touch of his hands and when the noise of doomsday receded for a moment, as the sea recedes before a tidal wave, he would speak to you—

"We are quite safe. This ship has been here before. You have nothing to fear."

"I know, I know. Then wh-wh-why am I afraid?"

"The sight, the sound, the being in the middle of an ultimate reality . . . they stupefy. The senses are overloaded and the mind retreats for its own protection. Those artists are accustomed to an abnormally high data input. They are born for it. And I—I admit I flinch, I am daunted; but life has made me rigid, I have learned how to exclude. You are shielded in neither way. It is nothing to be ashamed of, and it will pass. You should not be here watching."

"I must, I must."

"I can guess why. And you have been anxious of late, gnawing on your own nerves. That too has lowered your defenses against this—this spectacle which is at once psychedelic and terrorizing. I do not know why you should be unhappy, when everything seems to be going well for you—for the entire human race—"

A firefall thunders past. You hold to your solitary friend and babble, it matters not what, you reach out to him and you share.

For an instant he is like an iron bar. Afterward he eases, he continues to soothe, until the ship has rounded the sun and your lover can take you back to your cabin.

His room was so quiet that he could hear how his ears still rang from the violence he had survived. The room was empty, too, a cell for sleeping and nothing else, except that he had propped her picture before him as a

tiny brave splash of color against bareness. His tunic stank
from sweat, was hot and rough and tight around his neck.
He wanted to take it off, wash it, and not put it back on;
but he didn't.

He moistened his brush, passed the tip across an
inkblock, and wrote, taking as much time over the calligraphy as the composition:

My beloved daughter,
When you read this, if ever you do, you will be a young
lady, beautiful, gracious, generous with laughter, everywhere creating for yourself a world of dear friends. And I
will be dead, or I will be old and still more dour and
unbending than I am now. What will I have to do with
you? I am the daddy of little P'ing, who will have no
other way to welcome me when I come home than to
seize my thumb and stump off into the garden and maybe,
maybe call me a great big bag of love. But of Made-
moiselle Wang, what can I hope to be except the honor-
able father who once in the past did a thing that is
remembered? And this is natural and right. In fact, I do
not think of myself as anything more than a beast of
burden which has to carry certain loads in order that the
new world may be built.

Please understand, I feel no self-pity. When I look upon
the poor hollow people of the West, who have nothing to
live for beyond their own lives, I know how fortunate I
am. After you have had children of your own, you *will*
understand. Nevertheless, may I reach across time for a
moment and touch you?

If ever you read this, you will have read the histories. I
want you, and you alone, to know how behind the platitudes was a man, who did not know what he really was
but who knew loneliness, confusion, fright, weakness—I
would like for you to know me. Therefore I have vowed
neither to amend nor destroy these words, crude though
they are, but leave them for you to have when you come
of age.

At this hour, the entire purpose of my being is that you
shall live that long.

Today we traversed hell. You will have read about our
voyage. Quite likely, to you the solar passage will be
commonplace, a thing one does, hand in hand with a
sweetheart on a passenger liner to Saturn. But I saw hell.
Creation also, and that which calls the first foolish snow-
drop into bloom before winter has ended. But hell, I say

hell, the same that could in a single firetongue lick devour
my Blossom . . . though it might as easily carry her to the
enlightenment of beauty which has been mine.

Stunned, in panic, a person whom I sought to help let
slip to me—I do not believe she remembers she did—
that now the imperialists have this power to destroy
you. I had hoped— No matter. Twice they have broken
their most solemn oath. There shall not be a third time.
I go to do whatever is necessary.

That is my duty to mankind. My clumsy confession,
P'ing, is that this is only a pretense, and what I do is really
my love-gift to you.

He wondered whether to sign "Daddy" or "Your Father," decided on the more dignified form, read the page
through, folded and sealed it. Meanwhile he thought,
nausea binding his throat: *Is there any reasonable doubt
that my government is the one which hunted Yvonne
Canter?*

From his baggage he extracted the recoilless magnum
automatic that General Chou had insisted he bring. Chou
had been right.

Perhaps Wayburn and Canter would decide to do nothing, say nothing. It was not a chance to be taken. The
fact was that they had said nothing to him. The single
certainty was that Chou had no reason to pass the sun's
flame across Peking.

Wang checked magazine and action, put the gun in a
shoulder holster beneath his tunic, and left the gripper on
the garment loose so he could quickly reach inside. He
stowed the letter among his sparse effects and went forth
to spy out the situation.

XV

———◆———

"I'm sorry I was hysterical."

"I'm sorrier I ignored you. Let's forget it. We were both zonked out of our skulls."

Their bodies said the rest. Afterward they sought the food device. "Program for steak and French fries," Skip demanded. "If you want something exotic in addition, okay, but I need nourishment!"

Yvonne's laugh was tender. She made the appropriate passes, watching the resultant diagrams and refining her orders accordingly until they should have converged on the precise menu and production could commence. (Mammalian flesh, type bovine, 1.5 kilogram, dimensions ..., texture ..., degree of heat denaturing ..., temperature ..., flavor overtones ...) By now expert, she did the task quickly while letting her mind wander.

"A few short days," she said, "and we're home."

"Uh-huh. We better get in a lot of preliminary relaxation. Things'll be hectic for a while, groundside, 'Course, I suppose if we're rude we can protect ourselves somewhat, but— Oh, hi, Prof."

Yvonne's hair rippled as she turned to look. "Good evening," she said. "Would you like to join us for dinner?"

Wang stood straight. His lips barely moved, nothing else did in his face except a tic at the right corner of the mouth: "Are you feeling better?"

"Fine, thank you," she told him. "I only needed two or three hours of rest and—and recreation, and I bounced right back." She smiled with real warmth. "I might not have done this well except for you."

"Where is the Sigman?" Wang's tone was hoarse and strained.

"I dunno," Skip said. "Prob'ly catching its equivalent of a nap. Anything urgent?"

"Yes." Wang made as if to scratch beneath his tunic.

150

The uncharacteristic gesture brought both their gazes astonished upon him. Then the gun was out and he said: "Raise your hands. Do not move."

"What the devil—?" Skip grabbed toward the waistband of his shorts. Yvonne uttered a shriek.

"No!" Wang shouted. "Stand fast or I kill her!"

Skip lifted his arms. He had seen that kind of determination before. His heart thuttered, sweat broke forth, its acridity pierced the soft wet odors in the Sigman air. On his right he heard the breath move raggedly in and out of Yvonne.

"Good," Wang said. "Now listen. I am an expert marksman, and this pistol has no kick. There are eight bullets in the magazine and one in the chamber; I assume you know the type. Seven of those cartridges are magnum loaded. Hydrostatic shock alone would kill you instantly on impact. The first two are minim. They would disable you, Mr. Wayburn, for example by shattering a kneecap, but leave you fit to execute my orders. Dr. Canter is my hostage for your obedience."

Skip thought, *Stay calm, stay loose. Watch your chance, but for everything's sake don't try any heroics. Behind that iron mask, he's on the point of amok. See how the sweat is running out of him too!* He willed his lungs to stop gasping, his muscles to stop quivering and start easing. He did not quite have command of his voice: "What do you want?"

"To control this ship," Wang said. "You were shown how, and did not tell me."

"Huh? I—I never—"

"Be still. In her frantic condition, Dr. Canter blurted the truth to me."

"*No!*" Yvonne's scream came as if she were being flayed. She sank to her knees and brought hands up to cover her wild weeping.

"Do not blame yourself much." Wang's speech continued flat. "Blame me for taking advantage. Blame the Sigman for recklessly exposing creatures with whose psychology it was unfamiliar to extraordinary stress. Blame your lover for deserting you when you most needed him. First, last, and always, blame the fascists who did not keep faith. Because of them, I may no longer trust you. The issue is so great that trust in anyone except my country's leaders becomes treason to humanity."

"You fool," Skip said. He was faintly surprised at the composure his words now had. The coolness of crisis was

rising fast in him. "You're supposed to be a semanticist.
How can you think a swear word like 'fascist' means
anything, or using it solves anything? Did Vonny tell you I
wasn't going to let on?" *Or did she say what's true, that I
still haven't decided?*

Wang's monotone was dreadful to hear: "No, she merely let slip that you have the knowledge. The fact that you
kept silence before me speaks for itself. You may be a
man of essential good will. I rather believe you are. But I
must not make the assumption. The only mind I can read
is my own. Furthermore, if you were taught, others will
be, shortly after we reach Earth. Who is the first of them
and what does he do? I do not propose to gamble with the
future of several billion living human beings. They out-
weigh you two, Ahasuerus, and me by just that amount.

"We shall waste no more time. Conduct me to the
control room."

"We'd better obey, sweetheart," Skip said to the
crouched and crying woman. She didn't seem to hear.

"Assist her to her feet," Wang droned. "Keep your
hands in sight of me. I have watched you exercising and
know your capabilities."

Skip raised Yvonne. "Come along, robin." She hung on
him and keened. He bit his lip and slapped the bare back,
stingingly. She choked, then disengaged herself and
shuffled beside him, in advance of the gaping pistol
mouth.

"You will not be harmed needlessly," Wang said. "I will
have her bind you, secure her myself, and check your
bonds. I will care for you en route. On arrival, I will
inform the world that we are well but should be left
undisturbed for some hours until various preparations are
completed. Not that any terrestrial spacecraft can likely
lift off and make rendezvous sooner. They will have de-
tected us coming, but I will throw us into an unexpected
polar orbit. We will ride a tender to Peking. I will bring
back men and show them how to establish the invulnerable forcefield and pilot the ship. Then all will be well,
and you can probably be repatriated. If not, my influence
will assure you favorable treatment."

The corridors wound and intertwined, vivid with strange
murals. Leaves and flowers brushed skin and offered greet-
ings of bright perfume. The deck was springy under bare
feet. A sound like a gong beat through the moist warm
air.

"What's the Sigman doing meanwhile?" Skip asked.

"That must depend upon circumstances," Wang said. Earnestness tinged the machine voice: "Whatever is done is for his race too. When man and Sigman next meet, man must be peaceful. For that, we must first liberate him from his demons."

"Skip," Yvonne whispered, "oh, Skip, what can I say? What can I do?"

"Nothing," he responded. "You truly are not to blame. I love you."

They reached the command room. He had considered leading Wang on a snipe hunt, but the general location had always been fairly obvious. The bulkhead rose sheer and plain, except for some inset lenses and jutting force-projector snouts. "Give me a clear view of your procedure," Wang ordered. And the trouble was, the motions weren't delicate like the fingering out of a dinner. For a human—Ahasuerus had doubtless made adjustments —they were half a dozen simple wigwags.

The entrance dilated. Blackness lay beyond. "Dr. Canter goes through first," Wang said. When she entered, her body shone with a white light. It revealed the layout: a spherical chamber about five meters across, bisected by a transparent deck from which rose a number of stanchion rods. At the far end was a bank of the deceptively featureless boxes which housed the controls. "Next you, Mr. Wayburn," Wang said. "Go past Dr. Canter, to those instruments. She will stay near me."

The bulkhead closed behind them, and they stood surrounded by a sky image. This was a utilitarian place, and no attempt was made at perfect fidelity. The induced illumination from flesh and garments would have interfered anyhow. They saw the brightest and the nearest stars, though most of the latter are invisible to the naked eye. They saw the sun disc, and the lovely blue and gold companions which were Earth and Luna, and the trailing drive module. The sounds that elsewhere pervaded did not come here.

Wang posted himself beside the entrance. "Stand in front of me, Dr. Canter," he said. "Two meters or so off—do not obstruct my view—there. Mr. Wayburn, I was told that operation is similar to the boats', but I want a demonstration, plus a running description of what you do."

"That'll alert Ahasuerus," Skip said.

Wang nodded. "I know. Do not think to throw me down with an unheralded burst of high acceleration. I

have had Ch'an training; furthermore, I am used to travel
under the awkward and varying conditions of terrestrial
cosmonautics; and never forget that Dr. Canter's life depends on you."

Skip grimaced. *I can't get out of unlocking the controls;
and once he's seen how to do that, he could figure the rest
out for himself. Maybe the future does lie with the People's Republic.* He gesticulated. "This takes it off automatic. A repeat puts it back on."

"I see. Good. Let me think. ... Yes." Wang's left hand
closed on a stanchion in expectation of free fall. "Set us
on course for Mars. That should illustrate the principles."

Skip hooked a leg around a horizontal bar in front of
him and signed for a display. The airborne symbols were
easy to read. He directed the ship as he had been told,
explaining each step while he did. *No heroics. Nothing
that'll annoy him and kill her. Kill me, for that matter.
... I imagine the People's Republic will let us live, under
a kind of perpetual house arrest. Why not? But beloved
friends in the Byworld, what will become of you? Urania;
her boys; Rog Neal; Dan Keough; the Vikings who had
Earth's broad seas to roam in; Clarice—* And more and
more, hundreds he had met, thousands he had not, in
whom lay the hope of something new, not that return of
the almighty God-King which Wang Li thought was a
forward step—yes, and his parents, brothers, sisters, Vonny's kinfolk, the Almeidas, Thewlis, Kurland, more and
more of their kind too, what would become of them?

Meanwhile he brought the ship about. The change was
smooth. A period of weightlessness save for slight centrifugal force, while the dual modules rotated, was followed
by a resumption of linear acceleration, a vector combining
with present velocity to bring them to that planet named
for the lord of war. Nevertheless the Sigman would notice
and come aft.

"How do I explain to Ahasuerus?" Skip asked.

It made his spine crawl that the sweat beading Wang's
face and drenching his tunic should also shine white.
"Maybe Dr. Canter can help," the Chinese said.

"I don't know," she replied, scarcely to be heard. "If we
go forward to the synthesizer, maybe—"

"Let me doodle out that that's what we should do,"
Skip proposed.

"No!" Wang yelled. "How can I know what you are
telling it?" He swallowed. Monotone: "We must develop a
scheme which guarantees me against losing the upper

hand." The mask split in a wolf grin. "Not unlike the deterrence concept of the missile era—"

The bulkhead opened. Ahasuerus came in. All four eyes were out. Claws clacked. The scales glowed among the stars from which it had come.

Wang opened fire.

The reports smashed at eardrums. Two low-mass low-speed slugs rocked the Sigman. Wang backed toward the bulkhead, where he hid the image of Virgo, and fired the first of the magnums.

It crashed splintering through the armor, in among the naked cells. Juices spurted. Ahasuerus was flung off in a heap. It wailed, gathered itself and crept forward. Wang fired and fired. Each slug blasted more from the maker of beautiful things. Between shots, he waved the muzzle warningly across his prisoners. Yvonne clung to a stanchion and screamed as if she would never stop screaming. Skip turned his back.

After the fourth heavy blow, the Sigman could go no farther. Its deep-seated life was almost drained, in phosphorescent wetness that spread across the deck. It lifted a claw and chopped the arm through an arc. A gob of thick digestive fluid sailed past the Milky Way. It struck Wang on the breast and ate through cloth and inward. Ahasuerus collapsed in a rattle and sigh and was quiet.

Wang whimpered for pain. But his gun, however wobbling, remained in his grip. "I have . . . three bullets left," he said through clamped jaws. He pulled the tunic open, though the acids peeled flesh from the fingers of his left hand, and shrugged it off that arm. With the wadded sleeve he wiped the ulcer that gaped on his chest.

"I will live," he said shakenly. "The . . . wound is not mortal. The solvent seems to be . . . used up."

Skip approached, step by cautious step. "I'd better take a look," he said. Yvonne stumbled to him. He embraced her and whispered in her ear. She shuddered toward self-mastery.

"No," Wang said. "You will not . . . come any nearer."

"M-me, then," Yvonne stammered. "Let me help you." She clenched her fists, caught a breath, and went on: "If you feel you're about to faint—you'll kill us, won't you? Let me see what I can do to help you stay c-c-conscious. I'm a woman, no combat training, I couldn't hold you, you'd fling me aside and—"

"—and be prepared to shoot." Wang wheezed with the flame that was in him. "I am . . . not weakened, Wayburn,

not slowed ... not so much. You might reach me. You
could not get my weapon away in time to ... save
yourself."

"Agreed," Skip said.

Yvonne walked toward the pistol. She took Wang's
tunic gingerly by the collar. He pointed the muzzle around
her. "I must transfer this," he said. "To my left hand.
Before you can take my right sleeve off."

"Yes," she said.

She flung both arms about his wrist in the same motion
that threw her deckward. The pistol roared; a slug
whanged off the deck and the starry bulkhead. He tossed
her aside. Skip had bounded to him. He brought his gun
upward. If Skip seized him, Skip would take a bullet in the
back of the head.

The fang had been unleashed while the sigaroon did not
watch the murder of the Sigman. As he sprang, he drew it
from the rear of his waistband where he had stuck it. The
point went into Wang's throat, the edge slashed across.

Blood fountained over both men and Yvonne. Wang
fell. They thought they heard a noise from him like
"Yao—" Afterward was only a brief horrible bubbling;
and silence; and the blood of man and Sigman flowing
together on the deck and blotting out view of the Southern Cross.

XVI

—————◆—————

They had laid their dead near the hull portal, in the
room where first these met. Yvonne, clinging to Skip's arm,
said through tears, "We can't just launch them."

"Nor turn Ahasuerus over for dissection," he agreed.
"They rate a service, yes."

"Can we give them any? I mean ... do you know how
... in any faith, any tradition? I don't. A few bits and
pieces of Kaddish, of the Christian ceremony, vaguely
remembered from funerals—and when neither we nor
they believed— What have we to offer except pompous
made-up sentences?" She stared before her. "Nothing. It's
emptier in us than out yonder."

"I think they'd have liked the Wayfaring," he said.

"What?" She cast a blurry, bewildered look upon him.

"How my folk bury a friend. Nobody knows who wrote
the words, but most of us have learned them. 'Wayfarer,
farewell. For the gift of your love we thank you; and your
gift shall be cherished within us on every road we may
wander, and live between us in every camp where we
meet, and be given again when we likewise enter your
quietness. Until then we shall rejoice at sky, wind, water,
and wide lands, in your name and memory—' " Skip let
his voice trail off. "It goes on a short while longer," he
said shyly, "and we've got a particular way of setting
down wildflowers or what else can be had, and other such
customs. Do you think that'd be right?"

"Oh, yes, oh, yes," she said, and he could hear how her
misery was lifting. "We can take them to us, make them
belong— In the Byworld is our hope."

They stood on the observation bridge and watched
man's mother grow near. She shone cool blue amidst night
and stars. Clouds swirled white where rain went walking.
An ocean bore one incandescent point of sunlight. Offside

lay her moon, scarred and lifeless as if long ago it had felt the wrath of bombs; but men were there now, and in a few of their shelters grew roses.

"Ahasuerus loved Earth," Skip said.

"Wang Li did too," Yvonne answered.

He nodded. "We'll see if we can keep it for them." And then: "No. I shouldn't've spoken like that. The world's had overmany saviors and guardians."

Because of whom, his thought said, *two that we traveled with are on a straight-line orbit into the sun.*

But grief had faded, as it must and should, in those days he and Yvonne had added to their journey, laying their plans and making certain they could handle the ship.

The room was still. They had turned off the murmurous background, which was too reminding. Gradually they would learn how to make the ship sing of Earth. The atmosphere remained thick, warm, wet, and odorous, for they did not want to risk destroying their gardens. But they meant to move these into special places, and create through most of the hull an air better suited to them and to blossoms more familiar.

"Are you sure we'll able to control events that well?" she had asked when first they talked about the future.

"No," he said. "In fact, I doubt it. However, I am sure we've seen an end to grabbing and tearing after this power that ought to be only for—for—"

"For enlarging the spirit."

"Okay." He ran fingers through his hair while pacing before her. "It's ours. Yours and mine. We'll never give it to the Ortho. Anybody's Ortho. They had their chance and proved they aren't fit. Now let them whistle. We can't be touched. If necessary, we'll head outward. I know about a planet or two we could homestead. But I reckon we'd rather stay. And I'm fairly confident we can strike a bargain. Even one that'll let us visit Earth, immune from reprisals. Don't forget, we're uncatchable also in a tender. And we do have a lot to dicker with, like being able to ferry scientists. Of course, we'd better keep our people always in the majority aboard."

"Who are they?"

"Byworlders. Those I know personally, the right kind, gentle adventurers who've got no interest in running anybody else's life." He halted, squeezed her shoulder, and smiled down at her where she sat. "Maybe you'll pick a few Orthians like yourself. Fine. The point is, after they sign on with us, they're of the Byworld too."

The talk had been in their cabin, so his sweeping gesture had been at walls. But he meant the cosmos beyond.

The vision glowed from her. "And *we'll* keep the peace," she said.

"No!" he replied. "Don't you see, darling, that's been the whole trouble? That people have power over other people, or want it, or are afraid others want it? Ahasuerus didn't come here to put a new yoke on human necks."

"I'll have to learn your way of thinking," she said humbly. "To me it seems impossible that someone, someday, after we are gone, won't use the strength he'll have— for the highest purposes, with the best of intentions—"

His ardor waned. "A chance we can't escape taking. I'd sort of hoped that by then the race 'ud be spread far enough that nobody could rule it. But the more I think about duplicating this ship inside a thousand years, the crazier the idea looks."

Her turn came. She sprang to her feet and embraced him. "No, of course, dearest! I was being stupid. I ought to have realized immediately, considering how many technologists I've met— Listen, there're no secrets in nature. The question is simply whether or not a job can be done. If they know it can, that's clue enough. They'll find a way. And don't you think they'll put everything they have into it on Earth—when we are aloft to lure them? We can let trustworthy scientists make studies too. Skip, you like to bet. Will you bet me we won't live to see the first human starcraft—crude, maybe, but starcraft—depart for Sigma Draconis?"

He had gusted out a small, shaky laugh. "No, the odds look too long against me." At ease once more: "Unless the stakes are something I won't mind paying?"

—Now she spoke aloud, as if already her kindred could hear: "You'll get your chance. You'll go your thousand-fold ways, finding a hundred that are new and good, because we have the wisdom to see that nobody has the wisdom to tell the whole world what it must do."

"Aw, don't preach at them," Skip said. "Me, I lay no claim to a noble soul. I only figure to spend the rest of my life among the planets and maybe the stars, having an absolute ball."

Yvonne flushed. "That was sententious, wasn't it? I still haven't properly learned to be just myself. Will you keep showing me?"

He hugged her, between Earth and the Magellanic Clouds. "You know," he said, "that problem of ours, how we could stay together, we haven't found a solution and we never will. We'll never need to."

A while later he said, "I'd better stroll aft and conn us into orbit. Remember, in spite of criticism, I'm holding you to your promise that you'll compose our message to the people."

The Worlds of Poul Anderson is a special publication of The Gregg Press Science Fiction Series, a major Publishing program offering authoritative quality editions of the best in science fiction. Edited by David G. Hartwell and L. W. Currey, the series includes many classic works of science fiction and fantasy that have never before been published in hardcover editions. For further information about The Gregg Press Science Fiction Series, please inquire at your SF bookstore or library or write to Gregg Press, 70 Lincoln Street, Boston, Massachusetts 02111

Other Works by Poul Anderson
Available in Gregg Press Editions

The People of the Wind (Gregg Press, 1977). With a New Introduction by Sandra Miesel. This novel is central to the development of Anderson's interstellar trader and future history series (also known at the Technic Civilization Series) which began in 1958 with *War of the Wing-Men*. Nominated for both the Hugo (1974) and Nebula (1973) Awards, this is the first hardcover edition of one of Anderson's major works.

War of the Wing-Men (Gregg Press, 1976). With New Introductions by Charles N. Brown and Sandra Miesel. Not only the first novel in Anderson's Technic Civilization Series, this is also his first attempt to create a complex planet to use as a background. The novel also introduces the character Nicholas Van Rijn, a fat, jovial, ruthless merchant prince, who uses all his cunning to get help for his fellow humans marooned on Diomedes, and in the process he incidentally ends a war and improves Diomedian civilization.